PENGUIN BOOKS

TIME TRAVEL AND PAPA JOE'S PIPE

Alan Lightman is a physicist at the Smithsonian Astrophysical Observatory and teaches astronomy at Harvard University. His essays on science have appeared in *Science 86*, *Smithsonian*, *The New Yorker*, *The New York Times*, *Harper's*, and other publications. He was educated at Princeton and at the California Institute of Technology and lives in Concord, Massachusetts, with his wife and daughter.

TIME TRAVEL AND PAPA JOE'S PIPE

Alan Lightman

with ten illustrations by Laszlo Kubinyi

PENGUIN BOOKS

PENGUIN BOOKS
Viking Penguin Inc., 40 West 23rd Street,
New York, New York 10010, U.S.A.
Penguin Books Ltd, Harmondsworth,
Middlesex, England
Penguin Books Australia Ltd, Ringwood,
Victoria, Australia
Penguin Books Canada Limited, 2801 John Street,
Markham, Ontario, Canada L3R 1B4
Penguin Books (N.Z.) Ltd, 182–190 Wairau Road,
Auckland 10, New Zealand

First published in the United States of America by
Charles Scribner's Sons 1984
Published in Penguin Books 1986

Essays in this book have been published in the following publications: "Time Travel and Papa Joe's Pipe" and "I = V/R"
in *Smithsonian,* "The Space Telescope" in *The Boston Globe
Magazine.*

All other essays appeared in *Science 82, Science 83,* or *Science 84*
except "Students and Teachers" and "Mirage," which have not
been published before.

LIBRARY OF CONGRESS CATALOGING IN PUBLICATION DATA
Lightman, Alan P., 1948–
Time travel and Papa Joe's pipe.
Reprint. Originally published: New York:
Scribner, © 1984.   Includes index.
1. Science.   I. Title.
[Q171.L64   1986]   500   86-2573
ISBN 0 14 00.9212 9

Printed in the United States of America by
R. R. Donnelley & Sons Company, Harrisonburg, Virginia
Set in Bembo

Contents

Preface

Some years ago an old friend mesmerized me after dinner with his collection of paintings and illustrations by Maxfield Parrish. Parrish used a tedious and time-consuming technique called glazing, in which the artist begins with a white background and then adds successive layers of pure color, clear varnish, color, varnish, and so on—the aim being to mix light instead of pigment. Each stage of this procedure is methodical and familiar, but the final colors, fashioned from light that has shone down through the layers and reflected out again, are unlike any colors of this world. That is the magic of Maxfield Parrish. It is also the magic of science, placing one careful and logical step after another, yet eventually leading us into a realm we could not have imagined, where philosophy, art, and the human psyche filter the light. With these essays, I have attempted to explore that larger world. My perspective is that of a scientist, but I have let my mind wander, and I have seldom taken the same path twice. In blending the technical with the poetic, the cosmic with the down-to-earth, I have tried to reveal the human side of science. In these reflections of the universe, I hope my readers catch glimpses of themselves.

I want to express my gratitude to the people who helped me toward this book. First is my friend and poet Lucile Burt, whose wise and sensitive editorial advice strengthened every essay. Henry Abarbanel, Martin Carr, Jim Cornell, Dudty Fletcher, Madeleine Jacobs, Don Lamb, Beatrice Shube, and Kip Thorne encouraged me from the beginning and buoyed my spirits when it mattered. In David Roe, who visited Harvard for a year during this project, I found a needed kindred spirit. I thank my colleagues at the Harvard-Smithsonian Center for Astrophysics for helping me think through an occasional technical point. Don Moser and Jack Wiley at *Smithsonian* magazine graciously accepted my first essays for publication. I thank the excellent staff at *Science 84*, especially my personal editor Bonnie Gordon and editor-in-chief Allen Hammond, for their invitation to write regularly for that magazine and for their subsequent editorial guidance. Michael Pietsch, my editor at Charles Scribner's Sons, helped shape the overall balance of this collection and provided gentle but sure-handed editorial advice. Finally, I thank Jean, dear wife and artist, who inspired everything and constantly campaigned for a people-oriented approach; and my parents, who quietly filled our childhood home with art, music, history, and science, in which all things were possible.

Time Travel
and Papa Joe's Pipe

When astronomers point their telescopes to the nearest large galaxy, Andromeda, they see it as it was two million years ago. That's about the time Australopithecus was basking in the African sun. This little bit of time travel is possible because light takes two million years to make the trip from there to here. Too bad we couldn't turn things around and observe Earth from some cozy planet in Andromeda.

But looking at light from distant objects isn't real time travel, the in-the-flesh participation in past and future of Mark Twain's Connecticut Yankee or H. G. Wells's Time Traveler. Ever since I've been old enough to read science fiction, I've dreamed of time traveling. The possibilities are staggering. You could take medicine back to fourteenth-century Europe and stop the spread of plague, or you could travel to the twenty-third century, where people take their annual holidays in space stations.

Being a scientist myself, I know that time travel is quite unlikely according to the laws of physics. For one thing, there would be causality violation. If you could travel backward in time, you could alter a chain of events with the knowledge of how they would have turned out. Cause would no longer always precede effect. For example, you could prevent your parents from ever meeting. Contemplating the consequences of that will give you a headache, and science-fiction writers for decades have delighted in the paradoxes that can arise from traveling through time.

Physicists are, of course, horrified at the thought of causality violation. Differential equations for the way things should behave under a given set of forces and initial conditions would no longer be valid, since what happens in one instant would not necessarily determine what happens in the next. Physicists do rely on a deterministic universe in which to operate, and time travel would almost certainly put them and most other scientists permanently out of work.

But even within the paradigms of physics, there are some technical difficulties for time travel, over and above the annoying fact that its existence would altogether do away with science. The manner in which time flows, as we now understand it, was brilliantly elucidated by Albert Einstein in 1905. First of all, Einstein unceremoniously struck down the Aristotelian and Newtonian ideas of the absoluteness of time, showing that the measured rate at which time flows can vary between observers in relative motion with respect to each other. So far this looks hopeful for time travel.

Einstein also showed, however, that the measured time order of two events could not be reversed without relative motions exceeding the speed of light. In modern physics the speed of light, 186,000 miles per second, is a rather special speed; it is the propagation speed of all electromagnetic radiation in a vacuum, and appears to be nature's fundamental speed limit. From countless experiments, we have failed to find evidence of anything traveling faster than light.

There is another possible way out. In 1915 Einstein enlarged his 1905 theory, the Special Theory of Relativity, to include the effects of gravity; the later theory is imaginatively named the General Theory of Relativity. Both theories have remarkably survived all the experimental tests within our capability. According to the General Theory, gravity stretches and twists the geometry of space and time, distorting the temporal and spatial separation of events.

The speed of light still cannot be exceeded locally—that is, for brief trips. But a long trip might sneak through a short cut in space created by gravitational warping, with the net result that a traveler could go between two points by one route in less time than light would require by another route. It's a little like driving from Las Vegas to San Francisco, with the option of a detour around Death Valley. In some cases, these circuitous routes might lead to time travel, which would indeed raise the whole question of causality violation.

The catch is that it is impossible to find any concrete solutions of Einstein's equations that permit time travel and are at the same time well behaved in other respects. All such proposals either require some unattainable configuration of matter, or else have at least one nasty point in space called a "naked singularity" that lies outside the domain of validity of the theory. It is almost as if General Relativity, when pushed toward those circumstances in which all of physics is about to be done away with, digs in its heels and cries out for help.

Still, I dream of time travel. There is something very personal about time. When the first mechanical clocks were invented, marking off time in crisp, regular intervals, it must have surprised people to discover that time flowed outside their own mental and physiological processes. Body time flows at its own variable rate, oblivious to the most precise hydrogen maser clocks in the laboratory.

In fact, the human body contains its own exquisite timepieces, all with their separate rhythms. There are the alpha waves in the brain; another clock is the heart. And all the while tick the mysterious, ruthless clocks that regulate aging.

Nowhere is the external flow of time more evident than in the space-time diagrams developed by Hermann Minkowski, soon after Einstein's early work. A Minkowski diagram is a graph in which time runs along the vertical axis and space along the horizontal axis. Each point in the graph has a time coordinate and a space coordinate, like longitude and latitude, except far more interesting. Instead of depicting only where something is, the diagram tells us when as well.

In a Minkowski diagram, the entire life history, past and future, of a molecule or a man is simply summarized as an unbudging line segment. All this on a single piece of paper. There is something disturbingly similar about a

Minkowski diagram and a family tree, in which several generations, from long dead relatives to you and your children, move inevitably downward on the page. I have an urgent desire to tamper with the flow.

Recently, I found my great grandfather's favorite pipe. Papa Joe, as he was called, died more than fifty years ago, long before I was born. There are few surviving photographs or other memorabilia of Papa Joe. But I do have this pipe. It is a fine old English briar, with a solid bowl and a beautiful straight grain. And it has a silver band at the base of the stem, engraved with three strange symbols. I should add that in well-chosen briar pipes the wood and tobacco form a kind of symbiotic relationship, exchanging juices and aromas with each other, and the bowl retains a slight flavor of each different tobacco smoked in the pipe.

Papa Joe's pipe had been tucked away in a drawer somewhere for years, and was in good condition when I found it. I ran a pipe cleaner through it, filled it with some tobacco I had on hand, and settled down to read and smoke. After a couple of minutes, the most wonderful and foreign blend of smells began wafting from the pipe. All the various tobaccos that Papa Joe had tried at one time or another in his life, all the different occasions when he had lit his pipe, all the different places he had been that I will never know—all had been locked up in that pipe and now poured out into the room. I was vaguely aware that something had got delightfully twisted in time for a moment, skipped upward on the page. There *is* a kind of time travel to be had, if you don't insist on how it happens.

I = V/R

I was somewhat embarrassed not so long ago when I opened a year-old physics journal and read that two Japanese fellows had attacked the same problem I was currently finishing up, obtaining an identical solution. The problem, not so consequential now as I reflect stoically on my preempted calculations, concerned the spatial distribution that would eventually be achieved by a group of particles of different masses interacting with each other by gravity.

The underlying theories of gravity and of thermodynamics necessary for solving such a problem are certainly well established, so I suppose I should not have been surprised to find that someone else had arrived at similar results. Still, my pulse raced as I sat with my notebook and checked off each digit of their answers, in exact agreement with mine to four decimal places.

After doing science for a number of years, one has the overwhelming feeling that there exists some objective reality outside ourselves, that various discoveries are waiting fully formed, like plums to be picked. If one scientist doesn't pick a certain plum, the next one will. It is an eerie sensation.

This objective aspect of science is a pillar of strength and, at the same time, somewhat dehumanizing. The very usefulness of science is that individual accomplishments become calibrated, dry-cleaned, and standardized. Experimental results are considered valid only if they are reproducible; theoretical ideas are powerful only if they can be generalized and distilled into abstract, disembodied equations.

That there are often several different routes to a particular result is taken as an indication of the correctness of the result, rather than of the capacity for individual expression in science. And always there is the continual synthesis, the blending of successive results and ideas, in which individual contributions dissolve into the whole. Such strength is awesome and reassuring; it would be a tricky business to land a man on the moon if the space ship's trajectory depended on the mood of the astronauts, or if the moon were always hurrying off to unknown appointments.

For these same reasons, however, science offers little comfort to anyone who aches to leave behind a personal message in his work, his own little poem or haunting sonata. Einstein is attributed with the statement that even had Newton or Leibniz never lived, the world would have had the calculus, but if Beethoven had not lived, we would never have had the C-minor Symphony.

A typical example of scientific development lies in the work of the German physicist Georg Simon Ohm

(1789–1854). Ohm was no Einstein or Newton, but he did some good, solid work in the theory of electricity. Coming from a poor family, Ohm eagerly learned mathematics, physics, and philosophy from his father. Most of Ohm's important research was done in the period 1823–1827, while he worked grudgingly as a high school teacher in Cologne. Fortunately, the school had a well-equipped physics laboratory. In 1820 Hans Christian Oersted had discovered that an electric current in a wire could affect a magnetic compass needle, and this development impassioned Ohm to begin work in the subject. In those days electrical equipment was clumsy and primitive. Chemical batteries, invented in 1800 by Alessandro Volta and known as voltaic piles, were messy affairs, consisting of ten or more pairs of silver or copper and zinc disks separated by layers of moist cardboard. Ohm connected a wire to each pole of a voltaic pile and suspended above one of the wires a magnetic needle on a torsion spring. This was a crude device, operating on Oersted's principles, which could measure the current flowing through a wire. Ohm then completed the circuit by inserting test wires of various thicknesses and lengths between the two battery leads, measuring how the current changed and depended on the properties, or "resistance," of each test wire.

This initial work was done inductively, by the seat of the pants. Ohm published his results in a semiempirical form, smacking of the flavor of the laboratory. Some of the quantitative expressions of experimental data in the first paper in 1825 are actually slightly incorrect. This was soon to be rectified, however, for Ohm was enamored of the elegant and mathematical work of Jean Fourier on heat conduction and recognized some striking similarities to current flows. Under this influence, Ohm further developed and recast his results into more general mathematical expressions, not exactly matching his data but cleaving to the analogies with Fourier's work, a creative and crucial step.

The final results, stating in part that the current is directly proportional to voltage and inversely proportional to resistance (now universally known as Ohm's Law), were codified in an abstract and well-manicured paper published in 1827, very distant from those late nights with jumbles of wires and repeated exhortations to the voltaic pile to hold steady on the voltage.

When the complete theory of electromagnetism was assembled by James Clerk Maxwell in 1864, Ohm's work was deftly stitched in, like a portion of a giant tapestry. In 1900 Paul Drude published the first microscopic theory of resistance in metals, giving at last a satisfying theoretical understanding of Ohm's Law. Today we use Ohm's Law routinely in designing electrical circuits, in calculating how deep a radio wave will penetrate into the ocean, and so on. But there is little of Ohm in the abstract statement $I = V/R$ (Current equals voltage divided by resistance).

Max Delbrück, the physicist-turned-biologist, said in his Nobel Prize address, "A scientist's message is not devoid of universality, but its universality is disembodied and anonymous. While the artist's communication is linked forever with its original form, that of the scientist is modified, amplified, fused with the ideas and results of others and melts into the stream of knowledge and ideas which forms our culture." Perhaps if Georg Ohm had been a painter or a poet, we would now be celebrating his leaky voltaic pile, his uncalibrated galvanometer, his exact arrangement of odd wires and mercury bowls, or reliving the loneliness of his bachelor nights, his emotions and thoughts during the experiments.

It seems to me that in both science and art we are trying desperately to connect with something—this is how we achieve universality. In art, that something is people, their experiences and sensitivities. In science, that something is nature, the physical world and physical laws. Sometimes we dial the wrong phone number and are later found out. Ptolemy's theory of the solar system, in which the sun and planets revolve about the Earth in cycles and cycles within cycles, is imaginative, ingenious, and even beautiful—but physically wrong. Virtually unquestioned for centuries, it was ungracefully detonated like a condemned building as soon as Copernicus came along.

Very well. Scientists will forever have to live with the fact that their product is, in the end, impersonal. But scientists want to be understood as people. Go to any of the numerous scientific conferences each year in biology or chemistry or physics, and you will see a wonderful community of people chitchatting in the hallways, holding forth delightedly at the blackboard, or loudly interrupting each other during lectures with relevant and irrelevant remarks. It can hardly be argued that such in-the-flesh gatherings are necessary for communication of scientific knowledge these days, with the asphyxiating crush of academic journals and the push-button ease of telephone calls.

The frantic attendance at scientific conferences has been referred to as a defense of scientific territoriality, a dead giveaway to our earthy construction. I think it is this and more. It is here, and not in equations, however correct, that we scientists can express our personalities to our colleagues, relish an appreciative smile, speculate on the amount of Carl Sagan's latest royalty advance, and exchange names of favorite restaurants. Sometimes I enjoy this as much as the science.

The Loss of the Proton

Deep underground in the Kolar Gold Fields of southern India, cloistered within 150 tons of iron, electronic
devices are silently waiting for signs of proton decay.
Physicists, aboveground, are also waiting. The proton, a
sacred cow of physics, is a subatomic particle long believed to be indestructible in isolation. But if recent theories are correct, all protons will ultimately disintegrate.
Luckily this is a rare event; otherwise, atoms and scientists
would long ago have evaporated into energy. According
to hopeful expectations, the quantity of iron in the Indian-
Japanese experiment, containing about 10^{32} protons (one
followed by 32 zeros), should produce roughly one proton
decay per month. This is far less frequent than a single
grain of sand out of all the beaches on Earth going bonkers
once a month. But it's worth waiting for.

Proton decay is predicted, even required, by "grand
unified theories" in physics. For more than fifty years we
have been slowly groping our way toward a single, ex-

quisite theory that places on an equal footing the fundamental forces and particles of nature, a Golden Rule that sums up all the other rules of conduct the subatomic particles live by. In such unified theories, where there are no aristocracies or privileged survivors, proton decay is perfectly natural. Scientists in India, France, Italy, the United States, and the Soviet Union are now pursuing the Holy Grail of proton decay in different experiments.

Other endeavors in physics, although engaging and important, seem tame by comparison. Even as an undergraduate, making my first shy acquaintance with physics in the quiet of the library, I understood that the object of the game was to get down to the bottom, to explain the swing of pendulums and the blue of the sky and everything else in terms of two or three basic ideas. You can wander around forever in the jungle of hydrodynamics or thermodynamic ensembles, but the precious mulch is down, down beneath the ferns, into the realm of fundamental forces and particles. I've always envied the elementary particle physicists, especially those working on grand unified theories.

As we understand it now, there are four fundamental forces of nature: the gravitational force, the electromagnetic force, the strong nuclear force, and the weak nuclear force. We're most familiar with the gravitational force, which holds us agreeably to the ground. The electromagnetic force, acting between charged particles, is responsible for among other things the transmission and reception of radio broadcasts. Not so evident in daily life are the nuclear forces. Hydrogen bombs release the energy of the strong nuclear force, which grips protons and neutrons together within the atomic nucleus. The weak nuclear force is involved in certain kinds of radioactivity.

These four forces act at the subatomic level and up. At present we must accept their differences as givens. A successful grand unified theory would *predict* these differences, synthesizing the four forces into a single force in the process. What could be more pleasing? If we find that nature respects such a theory, our human yearning for simplicity and understanding will be gratified in the most profound way. Never mind the scientific jargon. Something special is in the works.

What's the secret? Forces reveal themselves by the behavior of particles. Grand unified theories propose that differences among the four forces would disappear if only we could probe near enough to the particles experiencing the forces. Each subatomic particle—the quark, for example, three of which make up the proton—may have just one universal interaction with other particles. But a quark attracts friends, other subatomic particles, seemingly from nowhere. And these friends have friends. What you end up with is a little community surrounding the quark, and you can't get a straight answer about what a quark's really like because all the other guys are constantly jabbering and confusing things with their own interpretations. It is the inevitable baggage of friends that explains in detail how the single, pure force by which particles interact takes on the character of four separate forces. Incidentally, this unplanned picnic that springs up around subatomic particles is quaintly called the vacuum.

We get the inside story only when two particles happen to come close enough so they can exchange forces quietly, without being disturbed by the vacuum. Proton decay is infrequent because two quarks within a proton must wander extremely close to recognize that the various other particles into which the proton might disintegrate are acceptably in the family. In grand unified theories, all particles are related.

Recent unified theories, beginning with a seminal paper in 1974 by Georgi, Quinn, and Weinberg, are almost but not quite whole; the electromagnetic, strong, and weak nuclear forces are merged. A grand unified theory including the gravitational force still eludes us. What's needed is a mathematical restatement of gravity in the language of quantum mechanics, the description of matter at the subatomic level; and we continue to bruise ourselves at every attempt. But nobody's giving up on gravity.

One reason we're optimistic in our striving toward a unified theory is the proven success of the electroweak theory. Developed in the 1960s by Glashow, Salam, and Weinberg, this theory, a fragment of a unified theory, brought together the electromagnetic and weak nuclear forces under a single mathematical umbrella. The electroweak theory, at the time of its proposal, was a gut feeling, a wish conjured up with hardly a shred of experimental justification. For almost a decade it hung in the air like a beautiful vapor. A striking prediction of the electroweak theory was the existence of an electrically neutral particle associated with the weak nuclear force, a first cousin to the photon of the electromagnetic force. The unmistakable fingerprints of this new particle, the Z_0, began showing up in the middle and late 1970s. Glashow, Salam, and Weinberg shared the Nobel Prize in 1979.

Einstein, if he were here to enjoy recent progress, would chuckle softly. For the last decades of his life he

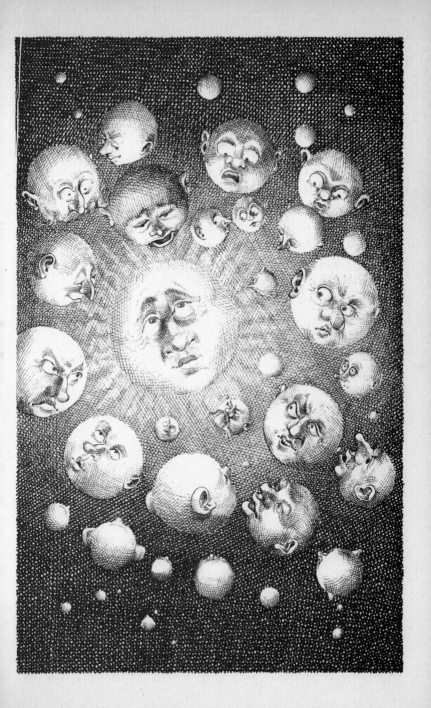

struggled to combine the electromagnetic and gravitational forces. His efforts were doomed, partly because he could never say yes to quantum mechanics. But Einstein knew what he was looking for. One way or another Einstein was always down beneath the ferns.

With each more complete theory, each new prediction like the Z_0 or proton decay, additional pieces of the big puzzle glide tentatively into place. In a fully unified theory every piece would fit, with none left over.

All this raises again the old idea, probably originating with the Greeks, that there may be only a limited number of fundamental laws of nature. If so, we could be hovering on the edge of Nirvana, scientifically speaking. Physicists, having at last found themselves and everything else in the process, would join hands in a giant circle, humming in unison the universal, omniscient, monosyllabic Om.

I hate to confess this, but I hope there's a snag along the way—a new kind of force or something we hadn't counted on. It's not that we won't still have plenty to do when and if a grand unified theory is confirmed. The fundamental laws of physics are like the rules for how pieces move on a chessboard; even with the rules in hand, we confront an enormous variety of complex and challenging situations.

But something will have been lost. Something that might stiffen our scientific creativity. Creativity is one of those magical things where you never know exactly what's happening under the hood. But whatever it is, I suspect it requires not knowing all the rules. We can, I think, continue to do quite well in science without having all the answers. Perhaps the poet Rilke meant something of this when he wrote that we should try to love the questions themselves, like locked rooms and like books written in a very foreign tongue.

Other Rooms

During the years I was preparing for a career in science, preoccupied with the autonomy of equations and instruments, human beings continually inserted their idiosyncrasies into my education. John, a boyhood friend and partner in early scientific adventures, first exposed me to the notion that success may arrive by a side-door approach. His gadgets worked and mine didn't. He never saved the directions that came with new parts, he never drew up schematic diagrams, and his wiring would wander drunkenly over the circuit boards; but he had the magic touch, and when he sat down, cross-legged, on the floor of his room and began fiddling, the transistors hummed. Watching over his shoulder in an attempt to discover why things worked in his house and not in mine was totally useless, nor was he able to explain anything. John didn't squander his time learning theory.

Afternoons, I would drop over from school with some idea I'd read in *Popular Science* or an interesting, scheme of my own and often find John stretched out and spindly on his bed, brooding over his most recent batch of poor grades. At the mention of a new project, with the barest shred of description from me, he would perk up and boost off, like a jazz musician transforming a ratty tune into a pulsing, living cascade of sound, never writing down a single chord. He'd instantly begin pulling electrical wires, soldering irons, chemicals, or whatever he thought was required from boxes piled here and there (in retrospect, my own room suffered from too much neatness) and, with the usual Bob Dylan record howling in the background, get down to business. Soon we'd be adrift, abandoning books, formulae, and schoolwork in favor of wonderful scientific devices, at great distance from the tiny voice of John's mother calling him to dinner.

Our most successful collaboration was a project we entered in the county science fair during my junior year of high school. It was a communication device, but the novel feature was the absence of electrical wires connecting transmitter to receiver and the use of light alone for encoding and transmitting sound. When a person spoke into the transmitter, the sound vibrated a stretched balloon, upon which was mounted a bit of silvered glass. Light originating in the transmitter and reflected from the little mirror thus carried along, through its variations in intensity, information about the original sound vibrations. This information was reconverted into sound by a photocell and amplifier at the receiver. For several months we had ravaged hardware and electrical supply stores around town and were intensely pleased with our final product. The day before the judging, after numerous and brilliant trials at up to 50 feet separation between talker and listener, something broke. I went home in a state of depression. Two days later I received an astonishing call from John saying that he had carried our stricken contraption to the fair late that night and craftily connected the transmitter and receiver with a wire run under the table. Next day the judges were fooled, apparently, and awarded us first prize. John was all practicality.

When I lived in Watertown, more than a decade later, a piano tuner named Phil used to come about every four months to spruce up our upright. Phil, I gradually learned, was just as theoretical as I but free of the nuisance of dressing his dizzy flights with scientific respectability. He was full of ideas about the origins of the universe, what might have come before, and other cosmological subjects. You could never tell, as he spun his fantastic monologues dancing back and forth between science and philosophy, which of his ideas he had read somewhere and which he was creating out of his head at that moment.

After his second or third visit, Phil somehow got wind of the fact that I was a physicist, which cemented our relationship and thereafter increased the tuning job from one to two hours. Upon his entrance into my apartment, Phil would briefly sound out the keys for about 15 minutes, as if on a dry run, and then disengage his bulky frame from the piano bench and begin spouting his latest theories. My favorite was one in which the solar system was really a big atom, at least as perceived by some giant, unspecified beings, and further out in space the galaxies formed a galactic solar system, which was really a galactic atom, and further out a number of different universes orbited each other. As Phil would describe this hierarchy of orbiting worlds, his voice increased appropriately, his gestures expanded into large arcs that narrowly missed the chandelier, and both of us would be irresistibly lifted up and away into outer space, my Watertown apartment and the entire neighborhood becoming a vanishing speck in the cosmos. Such fantasies would sometimes go on for half an hour. Phil had stamina. In the interlude where he caught his breath, I would sometimes come to my senses and attempt to inject some science into the discussion, drawing on my professional resources. After a fleeting look of worry, Phil would brush off this unwelcome bit of goatishness on my part and continue to greater heights.

On occasion, Phil had the facts exactly right, as far as I could tell, and my approving nod would bring forth a bright grin. One such time was his sobering description of how the continual creation and destruction of microscopic black holes distorts and punctures space, leading to a foamy structure at the most minute levels of reality. That day it took us nearly three hours to get the piano tuned, and I was late to the university.

During Phil's last visit, which was shortly before we moved, I had to immediately excuse myself to the study after letting him in, for I was behind in my research and had to make a presentation later in the day. Phil took this rather grumpily and, for a time, pounded the keys with unnecessary vigor. Without the intellectual excursions, in fact, he accomplished his work in a scant 60 minutes. As I sat working at my desk in the next room, Phil burst in without warning and, viewing the clutter of equations and books, said, "I see you do things the long way."

*　　*　　*

About a year later I learned with sadness that Jon Mathews, 48, a former professor of mine in graduate school, and his wife had been reported lost at sea while crossing the Indian Ocean alone in a 34-foot sailboat. Such an unkempt catastrophe simply could not be fastened onto other memories of Mathews, who was as meticulous in his scrubbed, crew-cut appearance as he was in his tidy mathematical calculations and who had seemed, at least to us students, to always look twice before leaping. Perhaps it was exactly his cautious and careful style that denied Mathews any truly outstanding contributions to his subject, theoretical physics. Something was missing, some touch of irreverence or deepness or momentary lapse of the rules. In a paper he is remembered for, titled "Gravitational Radiation from Point Masses in a Keplerian Orbit," Mathews begins, "One might expect masses in arbitrary motion to radiate gravitational energy. The question has been raised, however, whether the energy so calculated has any physical meaning. We shall not concern ourselves with this question here. . . ." and then goes on to do a textbook calculation of the conjectured effect. In fact, Jon was a superb teacher and a coauthor of the widely used textbook *Mathematical Methods of Physics*. At the blackboard he was in his element, distilling the physical world into beautifully chalked equations running on for many feet, explaining each concept in mechanics or electromagnetism so clearly and exactly that you could begin to see an equation on the board wiggle back and forth like the pendulums or springs it described. Jon was such a good teacher that some of us audited his courses without credit, forcing a space in our frantic graduate studies to hear a familiar subject discussed with elegance and precision. I became friends with Jon through our common love of sailing. Even then, years before his ill-fated voyage, he dreamed of one day sailing around the world, talked about it, and recruited eager students to serve as crew for weekend jaunts on his boat.

A cruise I remember was to Catalina Island, California, about 30 miles off the coast of Long Beach. Jon's wife Jean wasn't along, but one of his children was. Going out, we had a stiff and shifty breeze. Jon hustled around the boat with surprising agility, cranking winches, reefing the main, resetting pulleys, and generally in complete control, as calm as if he were solving a straightforward boundary value problem at the blackboard. His boat was immaculately kept, its brass hardware gleaming and in good repair, lines religiously coiled when not in use, and every item in its proper place—a rare state of affairs on sailboats. That night, at anchor off the island, with the boat gently rocking and us cozy in the cave-lit cabin within, Jon unwrapped his most recent toy to show me, a sextant, his voice pitched high as always when he was explaining something new. We never talked physics on board. I don't know why, we just never did.

The physicist Freeman Dyson has likened much of scientific research to craftsmanship, in which "many of us [scientists] are happy to spend our lives in collaborative efforts, where to be reliable is more important than to be original." That kind of science, even done well, was not enough for Jon. He pursued one hobby after another to complete himself, including an unexpected mastery of Eastern languages, revealed one day in his orderly office when he pulled down from the bookshelf a volume in Sanskrit and began reading to me.

This was all a decade ago. Little by little, Mathews garnered the necessary expertise, the many practice cruises, and the navigational and geographical knowledge to materialize his dream of sailing around the world. On his 1979–1980 sabbatical leave he set sail from Los Angeles in early summer, heading west. The last reported radio contact with him was in December 1979, several hundred miles from Mauritius. A friend was waiting in South Africa for his arrival, which never occurred. Mathews and his wife were apparently the victims of an Indian Ocean cyclone, the counterpart of hurricanes in the Caribbean or typhoons in the China Sea. The peak season for such storms in the Indian Ocean begins in December, and Mathews had planned his trip so that the crossing would take place well before. However, according to reports I've read, he was already behind schedule before reaching Australia and, rather than turn back or remain berthed for an additional six months while the storm season passed, decided to risk the crossing.

I have tried to recreate in my own mind what must have been happening in his, as Jon pondered charts and timetables and weather reports in Australia and then decided to take the biggest gamble of his life. I picture him as the storm first hit, suddenly finding himself out of control in a vast, raging place he'd never imagined, a room without walls or ceiling or solution. Jon's brilliant lectures in the classroom, his beautifully scripted Sanskrit, our fellowship within the watertight world of neatly stacked journals and equations pale beside that final image, that final search for completion.

Origins

When I was a child and asked my parents where I came from, they referred me to the copy of *The Stork Didn't Bring You* nestled in the den library, and that was that. While still in awe of the biological details, I became a physicist. Physicists, who by profession think in the simplest terms possible, have their own version of the story. Brushing aside questions of egg and cell development, evolution of the species, and so on, they get down to atoms in the body. A physicist's answer to where we came from is an investigation of the origins of the chemical elements. As it turns out, we were all made in stars, some 5 to 10 billion years ago.

All living matter we know about is composed mainly of hydrogen, carbon, oxygen, nitrogen, phosphorus, and sulfur. Carbon, with its rich variety of chemical bonds, is particularly suited for forming the complex molecules that life thrives on. Atoms of all these elements are continuously cycled and recycled over many generations through our planet's biosphere, incorporated into plants from the soil, swallowed by animals, inhaled and exhaled, evaporated from oceans, and returned to soil, air, and sea. We've been trading atoms with other living things since life began.

But where did the atoms come from? One rather bland possibility is that they were always here, in their observed proportions, thus putting a stop to further delicate questions. A great deal of scientific evidence, however, suggests this is not the case. First of all, the Earth is radioactive. Atoms of various elements are constantly aging and changing into other atoms by the ejection and transformation of protons and neutrons in their nuclei. For example, uranium 238, consisting of 92 protons and 146 neutrons, changes into thorium 234 by the simultaneous emission of two protons and two neutrons. Thorium is itself unstable and decays into another element and then another, until lead 206 is produced. Lead, at last, is mature, and the transformation process comes to a halt.

For years, chemists and physicists have been taking census reports of these busy families of atoms, with their noisy infants, teenagers, and quiet senior citizens. It seems perfectly natural that the relative proportions of the elements had to be different in the past. How far in the past? Analyses of the observed numbers of uranium versus lead atoms, for example, have determined that the Earth is 4.5 billion years old. Our atomic roots go back this far and further.

The best guide to what was happening so long ago is found in the vast reaches of space, beyond our solar system, beyond our galaxy of 100 billion stars, beyond our neighboring galaxies. When we peer out through our tele-

scopes at distant galaxies, hundreds of millions of light-years away, we find them receding from us. The universe is and has been in a state of expansion, with the galaxies rushing away from each other like painted dots on an expanding balloon. Running this scene backward in time suggests the universe began about 10 billion years ago, in an initial explosion called the Big Bang. At this point even the people who work on these things start getting wide-eyed, despite the logic of equations, computers, and telescopes.

The early universe was much denser than today's. And it was much hotter, just as squeezing an ordinary gas tends to raise its temperature. When the universe was sufficiently young and hot, none of the chemical elements except hydrogen 1 (whose nuclei are single protons) could have existed. The constituent protons and neutrons of any compound atomic nucleus would have simply evaporated under the intense heat. For example, carbon and nitrogen atoms would have disintegrated into unattached protons and neutrons at temperatures exceeding about 2,000 billion degrees Fahrenheit. According to cosmological theory, this was the case until a ten-thousandth of a second after the Big Bang. As far as we can tell, the infant universe held only a shapeless gas of subatomic particles. Atoms, stars, planets, and people came later.

With only some introductory thermodynamics, a little cosmology, and some whisperings from nuclear physics, we have narrowed down the origin of the elements to some time after the universe began but before the formation of the Earth. Where and when did this occur?

Results in nuclear physics indicate that, starting from a hot gas of unattached protons and neutrons, synthesis of complex atoms proceeds along a family tree, in which heavier atoms grow from lighter ones. Since the temperature and density of the expanding, primeval universe were dropping rapidly with time, there was only a brief period, ending a few minutes after the Big Bang, when conditions were right for creating elements. Before this period, every partnership of two or more particles evaporated; after this period, the subatomic particles did not have the energy and were too far apart for fusion to occur easily. According to theoretical calculations, element formation in this delicate interval got only as far along as helium 4 (two neutrons and two protons), the lightest element after hydrogen. The predicted amount of helium produced, about 25 percent of the mass in initial protons and neutrons, is in delightful agreement with current-day observations of the cosmic helium abundance. Nice, but what about carbon, oxygen, and other elements?

The answer, as we now understand it, began emerging in 1920 when the eminent British astronomer Sir Arthur Eddington first proposed that the sun and other stars are powered by nuclear fusion reactions. This is the same source of energy that is unleashed, for ghastly purposes, in our hydrogen bombs. In the deep interior of stars, densities and temperatures can become sufficiently high to fuse lighter elements into heavier ones, going far beyond helium. Such observed features of stars as their masses, temperatures, and luminosities accord well with the theoretical models and provide indirect confirmation of the hypothesized nuclear reactions. These are the facts of life that adult physicists and astronomers will tell you.

More direct evidence for the element-producing activity of stars comes from analysis of the debris ejected by exploding stars. In such explosions, called supernovae, nuclear reactions proceed at an extremely rapid rate; both the hastily produced elements and those manufactured in the preceding, more leisurely evolution of the star are spewed out into space, where we can have a good look at them. Analyzing the telltale colors of light emitted by stellar ejecta reveals a host of heavy elements, in the relative proportions predicted by nuclear physicists.

The first stars could have begun forming long ago, when the universe was only a million years old. In fact, we see evidence for a great spread in the ages of stars. New stars are continually being born. Relatively young stars, like our sun, and its surrounding planetary system have condensed out of gas enriched with the drifting fragments of ancestral stars, gas thus enriched with heavy elements.

As we go about our daily business on this small planet, we have little feeling for the bond between us and those distant points of light. Excepting hydrogen and helium, all the atoms in us and our biosphere were bred somewhere in space, in the nuclear reactions of some now defunct star.

Nothing but the Truth

In a new preface to his first novel, Italo Calvino reminds us that writers mold reality to fit their purposes; landscapes are distilled, remembered faces are tortured. Art demands interpretation and recasting of the naked experiences of life. To some extent the same is true of science. Nature does not reveal herself in easy glimpses of scientific truths. Experimental results are often confusing and sometimes plain wrong. Without an interpretive theory, without a design offered by the beholder, observations of the physical world are just so many loose, meaningless facts.

Little wonder then that the history of science is replete with personal prejudices, misleading philosophical themes, players miscast. Prejudice is a dirty word in science, whose musty corridors were supposedly swept clean by Copernicus and Galileo. Yet I suspect all scientists have been guilty of prejudice at various times in their research.

An unexpected example can be found in the work of Lev Davidovich Landau, winner of the 1962 Nobel Prize in physics. Among other things, Landau made major contributions to the theories of ferromagnetism, super fluids and superconductivity, and suggested the fundamental law of charge-parity conservation. Landau pioneered the school of modern Soviet theoretical physics and was practically worshiped by colleagues. He was also feared, partly for his habit of ruthlessly ferreting out and destroying all unproven statements in scientific discussions. The nameplate on his office door at the Ukrainian Physicotechnical Institute read "L. Landau. Beware, he bites."

One of Landau's favorite remarks was "Nonsense always remains nonsense." In 1932, with several important pieces of work already under his belt, Landau published a curious three-page paper called "On the Theory of Stars." The paper begins with high expectations, quickens through its penetrating and elegantly simple calculations, and ends in nonsense.

What is shocking about the 1932 paper is that Landau, without warning and in a single sentence, dismisses a major branch of physics. The paper concerns a theoretical investigation of the structure attained by stars in balancing their inward gravitational forces against their outward pressure forces. For the burned-out stars Landau was considering, the outward pressure forces are prescribed by quantum mechanics, the theory of matter at the atomic level. By 1932 the laws of quantum mechanics had been firmly established and ranked beside Einstein's relativity as the foundation for modern physics. To Landau's dismay, his calculations predicted that burned-out stars cannot avoid complete inward collapse if slightly more massive than the sun. That is, in sufficiently massive cold stars no amount of internal pressure can counterbalance the inward crush of gravity, leading to a frantic contraction of the star from a sphere a million miles or more across down to a point. Landau then writes "As in reality such masses exist quietly as stars and do not show any such ridiculous tendencies, we must conclude that ... the laws of quantum mechanics are violated." (Sir Arthur Eddington made an almost identical remark at a Royal Astronomical Society meeting in 1935, upon reviewing calculations by S. Chandrasekhar that independently reached the same conclusions about cold stars.)

Landau had little justification for this statement. Puzzling, for such a meticulous scientist. Astronomers had indeed observed very massive stars quietly avoiding collapse, but these were clearly not the burned-out, cold stars Landau's calculations applied to. Hot and cold stars were, in fact, easily distinguished by their colors. In his mistaken reference to observed stars we see a mirror turned not outward to external reality, but inward. It seems Landau found his theoretical result (which was actually one of the first predictions of black holes) so preposterous, so disturbing to common sense, that he was willing to abandon the celebrated theory that produced the result. And in the same, concise prose that normally followed logically from his calculations.

Landau's paper was not the first example of personal prejudice in science, nor the last. In 1917 Einstein modified, in a completely ad hoc manner, his 1915 theory of gravity because it predicted a dynamic universe, a cosmos always on the move, either expanding or contracting. Since Aristotle, the stationarity and permanence of the universe had been simply accepted in Western thought, like night changing into day. There was certainly no observational evidence to the contrary. Einstein succumbed to this bias. Where his original equations were dispassionate, he was not. Einstein realized his mistake in 1929, when the astronomer Edwin Hubble looked at distant galaxies through a telescope and noticed that the universe was expanding.

Landau and Einstein might be forgiven for placing too much trust in their physical intuition. To the theoretician at the drawing board, reminiscences of physical reality are a valuable tool—an important distinction between science and mathematics. When totally unfamiliar results like black holes and expanding universes peer out from the equations, even fearless intellects sometimes retreat.

With observational science, personal bias can take a subtle form. In 1969 Joseph Weber of the University of Maryland reported positive evidence for the first detection of gravitational radiation, the weaker cousin of electromagnetic radiation and long predicted on theoretical grounds. In the subsequent decade other scientists repeated Weber's experiments with more sensitive equipment, but obtained only negative results.

In 1975 P. Buford Price of the University of California at Berkeley and collaborators announced evidence for the detection of magnetic monopoles. Magnetic monopoles, if they exist, would be the magnetic version of electrically charged particles, such as electrons, and would place electricity and magnetism on an equal footing. Many physicists have long been troubled by the apparent absence of magnetic monopoles. A theory for such particles has been in hand since 1931. But Price almost certainly misinterpreted his data, as later analyses by other scientists showed. Both Weber and Price were earnestly stalking their prey. In science, as in other activities, there is a tendency to find what we're looking for.

And it's not surprising. After a day in the laboratory with the purring instruments or the silent equations, scientists return to the world of other men and women. Listen in at a scientific conference while people are presenting the results of their research. If a scientist has given himself to the project, you'll hear more than summaries of data and procedures. Chances are you'll hear a lively commentator, an advocate of a particular point of view, a man or woman trying to make sense of things in their own terms. As Bacon shrewdly observed, "The human understanding is no dry light, but receives an infusion from the will and affections; whence proceed sciences which may be called 'sciences as one would.' For what a man had rather were true he more readily believes."

Fortunately, the scientific method, that legendary code of detachment and objectivity, does not hang on the actions of individual scientists. Instead, it draws strength from collections of scientists, experiments repeated to confirm or deny, theories considered and reconsidered by skeptics. Scientists may defend their own ideas with unseemly dedication, but they relish finding flaws in the work of colleagues. Most personal prejudices crumble under such an onslaught of devil's advocates.

There's another source of unbridled hypothesis from which science, even as a collective enterprise, is not immune. And that's the great distance between theory and experiment in some areas, leaving portions of theories adrift and stranded, without easy approach. Einstein's theory of gravity is well tested in the solar system, but it also makes critical predictions about black holes, where gravity is a million times stronger than at the sun. The debate in biology over gradual versus catastrophic change in evolution of species remains controversial partly because a decisive fossil data base is hard to come by. Scientific theories stand or come tumbling down on their predictions; when predictions outstride our ability to test them, we've entered dangerous territory. My own cautious prediction is that this will remain a problem we have to live with. Even in science, our minds can flutter to heights where bodies cannot follow.

Several years ago I heard a commencement address by Richard Feynman, a Nobel Prize winner who worked on some of the same problems as Landau. It was a warm June morning. The future scientists sat in folding chairs on the lawn, perspiring in their black gowns. But no one noticed the heat. Hundreds of young faces were fastened on the podium, where Feynman was giving advice. He said that when we do scientific research, when we publish our results, we should try to think of every possible way we could be wrong. His words hovered in the thick air, blending with the various ambitions and beliefs gathered there. It was a tall order.

Science on the Right Side of the Brain

How we think is not something we often think about. Even serious mental tasks don't require much understanding of the machinery perched up there. When we do think about the mind, it seems different from our other parts, a disembodied vessel out of which thoughts flutter. And the proposition of mind studying itself flounders in a certain catch-22 absurdity. It seems almost impossible that such an entity could exist as physical matter inside our heads, but that's exactly the point of view taken, with great success, in modern brain research. In fact, a revolution in neuroscience and its applications is now underway, taking place quietly beside all the commotion in computer technology and molecular biology.

A major development in neuroscience has been the gradual understanding of the different functions of the right and left halves, or hemispheres, of the brain. To the untrained eye the two halves may appear identical, but it is now believed that the left hemisphere is primarily responsible for logical, linear kinds of thought processes, including language and mathematical skills, while the right is responsible for spatial relationships and holistic processes, including artistic skills. Although the two sides cooperate in normal individuals, the degree of activity in each hemisphere varies from person to person and also from culture to culture.

These findings first began emerging in 1861, when Pierre Paul Broca localized the center of articulate speech in the left frontal cortex. Beginning in 1953, the subject advanced dramatically with the split-brain experiments of Roger Sperry and collaborators. Sperry worked with epileptic patients whose corpus callosum, the bundle of nerves connecting and allowing communication between the two hemispheres, had been surgically severed to reduce the intensity of seizures. Since each hemisphere controls and receives stimuli from only one side of the body, it then became possible to explore separately the two sides of the brain. In 1981 Sperry was awarded the Nobel Prize for his work.

It's always seemed obvious, without being clear in detail, that there are two different ways of approaching problems—the intuitive and the analytic. At different times one or the other approach works better, and most of us operate more comfortably in one mode or the other. Sitting at the extremes, at least in stereotype, are artists on the right and scientists on the left, both groups viewing the world at an angle. About 55 years ago Rudyard Kipling wrote the eerie poem "The Two-Sided Man," which begins, "Much I owe to the lands that grew/More to the Lives that fed/But most to the Allah Who/Gave me two separate sides to my head."

Having acknowledged the debts to Allah and to Sperry, how can we use all this to our advantage? An inspiring practical attempt is the recent book *Drawing on the Right Side of the Brain* by Betty Edwards. Edwards teaches art, and her thesis is that we can all learn to draw better by consciously holding at bay our left hemisphere with its preconceptions about what things *should* look like. The book gives many exercises aimed at distinguishing the handiwork of the separate hemispheres and at learning how to quiet down the interference from the left side so the right side can come out and play. My favorite exercise is one where you take a Picasso line drawing of a man sitting in a chair, turn it upside down, and copy what you see. It's crucial that you not turn the Picasso right side up during the exercise, the whole point being you're not supposed to recognize arms and chair legs and such things. Once a familiar object is identified you're in deep trouble, because the left side will take control and draw it the way you've always seen it before. I'm no artist, but after a tedious half hour, upon turning my strange jumble of lines right side up, I was astonished to see a rather nice and unstiff drawing of a man sitting in a chair.

Clearly, Edwards's book and its underlying ideas have meaning for any creative enterprise. I suspect that most scientists might profit by trying some of these exercises, perhaps in a different version. Traditional scientific training focuses almost entirely on mastering the established body of knowledge, getting an appreciation for the scientific method of critical evaluation and learning the necessary experimental and mathematical techniques. This is almost pure left-hemisphere stuff. However, there must often be an additional, intuitive factor in doing first-rate scientific work. Mendeleyev's periodic table of the chemical elements, pointing out the similarity of every eighth element in a sequence arranged according to increasing atomic weight, resulted from years of his own meticulous accumulation of data. However, he may have been influenced by John Alexander Newlands's Law of Octaves reported several years earlier. Newlands had somehow noticed the same chemical relationships with much less data.

My own christening with doing science on the right side of the brain occurred a decade ago. I was a graduate student in physics at Caltech and, after waffling around with course work for well over a year, had finally settled into some genuine research. My first couple of research projects were brief and tidy. Then I fastened onto a more open-ended investigation that, in its loftiness, held the disturbing possibility of leading me off into the trees. As it was a theoretical project, all my work took place within a tiny office, equipped only with a desk, books, pencils, and paper. There were no windows. It was another world in that office. Day after day, while Kissinger was announcing and unannouncing that "Peace is at hand" and Howard Hughes was hiding out on the nineteenth and twentieth floors of a Vancouver hotel, I sat quietly with my equations. Getting nowhere.

My project concerned the implications of the well-documented fact that, neglecting air resistance, all objects fall with exactly the same acceleration under the influence of gravity. A physicist at Stanford had conjectured that this experimental result required a very special mathematical description of gravity, and I was trying to prove or disprove his conjecture. Going over and over pages of

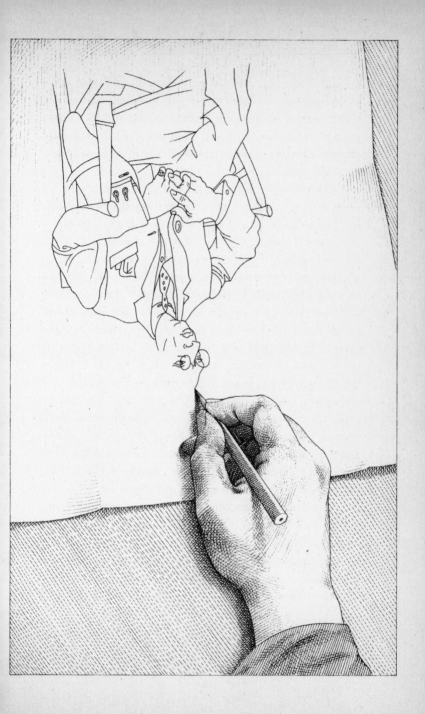

calculations, checking and rechecking each day, I knew something was amiss. An expected answer at the halfway point was not coming out right. Occasionally I ventured from my office for an outside diagnosis, but I soon realized gloomily that my colleagues couldn't help me. I was alone with the problem.

This went on for a couple of months. Then one day I found my mistake. And I knew immediately that the rest of the project would go without a hitch, yielding a yes to the conjecture. I don't know how I did it, but it wasn't by going from one equation to the next. Despite all attempts, I've never been able to retrace my steps on that day. My right hemisphere, I believe, had somehow got into the act, taking off into unknown territory. Other people have tried to describe that lifting feeling when everything suddenly falls into place. For me, the best analogy is what sometimes happens when you're sailing a round-bottomed boat in strong wind. Normally, the hull stays down in the water, with the frictional drag greatly limiting the speed of the boat. But in high wind, every once in a while the hull lifts out of the water, and the drag goes instantly near zero. It feels like a great hand has suddenly grabbed hold and flung you across the surface like a skimming stone. It's called planing.

I've planed in my scientific career only on a few occasions and then only for seconds. Einstein and Darwin probably planed for minutes at a time. The years of details at my desk have been bearable because of those moments. I could use a lot more of them. Perhaps, at just the right time, you have to glance at the equations upside down.

On the Dizzy Edge

Most scientists will tell you there is a clear line between science and philosophy, between those questions that are answerable by logic and experiment and those that must forever float in the nethers of epistemology. Such is the heritage of Bacon and Galileo. Following this comfortable approach, many of our finest biologists, chemists, and physicists have nestled into their numbers for the duration. And it's not surprising. In this strange and deep universe, humankind has an urgent desire to know some few things with certainty.

But the philosophers will not leave us our scattered harbors. Listen to the persuasive words of Bertrand Russell, philosopher and master logician: "The observer, when he seems to himself to be observing a stone, is really, if physics is to be believed, observing the effects of the stone upon himself." What can we know, if not the world of appearances? Adding to our anxieties, modern science, through no fault of its own, repeatedly brings itself right to the dizzy edge of philosophy.

An example, and one that makes me nervous every time I consider it, is the recent work suggesting that life could not have arisen anywhere in the universe if the values of certain physical parameters were somewhat different from what they actually are. One such parameter is the strength of the nuclear force that binds neutrons and protons within the atomic nucleus. If this parameter were slightly weaker, complex nuclei could not hold together. If it were slightly stronger, all nuclei would contain a minimum of several particles. In that case hydrogen, the lightest and simplest atom, would not exist. From all our experience in biology we believe that complex atoms, like carbon, as well as the simplest atom, which with oxygen makes water, are required for life forms. The nuclear parameter, like the speed of light, is a "fundamental constant" of nature, presumably the same always and everywhere in the universe. Although beyond our control, a slightly larger or smaller parameter would have eliminated our existence. Aren't we lucky it fits.

Another such parameter is the rate of expansion of the universe at the present epoch, about 10 billion years after the Big Bang. Ten billion years is the evolutionary lifetime of a typical star. We have good evidence that all complex atomic nuclei are synthesized in the violent interiors of stars. If the universe had a significantly smaller initial expansion rate, it would have recollapsed and ended in a reverse Big Bang long before now, long before stars could manufacture the chemical elements. With a somewhat larger expansion rate, however, the gravitational attraction of one bit of matter for another could never have sufficiently overcome the initial flinging apart to form clumps of mass like galaxies and stars. Since living structures apparently require complex atoms, and complex atoms were made in stars, the cosmological parameter in a life-supporting universe could not have been much different than it is.

Assumed fixed when the universe began, the cosmological parameter is called an "initial condition." Scientists routinely march forth from such givens. A more mundane example is the position at which you choose to release a frictionless pendulum. Once released, the pendulum swings to and fro according to the laws of physics, always rising to that initial height where the hand let go. Here the initial condition is controllable. In the cosmological example, it is not.

In addition to the nuclear and cosmological parameters, the values of several other unbudging parameters in physics, seemingly accidental, are found to be surprisingly constrained by the requirement that life evolve. The idea of these arguments is called the anthropic principle and was first introduced by Robert Dicke in 1961. *Anthros* is the Greek word for human. The analyses, however, have applications far exceeding human life. In the last decade the anthropic principle has been greatly extended by Brandon Carter and other respectable scientists.

Into all these arguments of course go assumptions about the nature and required conditions of life, and here we must not be too provincial. Copernicus taught us that our own peculiar planet is not the center of things. Perhaps life can thrive without such familiar stuff as water and carbon. Admittedly with regret, I would be willing to consider on paper a universe with very different parameters, a universe inhospitable to humans but bracing to gal-gols, composed of intelligent clouds of electrostatic energy. However, the anthropic principle, in its strongest form, states that no life whatsoever could exist anywhere or any time in the majority of possible universes. Before accepting this remarkable proposition, we must diligently seek out life forms very different from our own, including some definitely out-of-town types like the galgols.

Even with these cautionary remarks, the anthropic principle stares at us atop considerable scientific support, and we cannot look the other way. There are several possible explanations. One has courageously been proposed by physicist John Wheeler. Using as justification the unavoidable interaction between observer and observee dictated by quantum mechanics, Wheeler suggests that what we regard as fundamental constants have, in fact, been altered by our consciousness of them. In this view, life tapers the universe to fit its needs, through some unspelled-out process at the microscopic level. Another possibility, lying in the religious domain, is that some prime mover purposefully designed the initial conditions and parameters of the universe so that life would evolve. Still another possibility is that the existence of our particular life-supporting universe is simply an accident. Then it's only a question of statistical probabilities. Many other universes, with vastly different parameters, could easily have been in this one's place, and got along nicely without life forms evolving to ask embarrassing questions. Inconveniently, we have no other universes to compare.

Somehow, none of these explanations rescues me from my bewilderment. Wheeler's ideas imply something like a physical force associated with consciousness. (Perhaps force is not even an applicable concept.) But what could have been conscious in the unimaginable temperatures of the Big Bang? The arguments about a prime mover must be accepted or rejected on faith. And finally, it is profoundly insulting to consider all living things as resulting from a roll of the dice.

It's difficult to be alive and not to feel that, amid rocks and air and stars, something is special about life. But what? And why? What difference to the universe is our brief flicker of consciousness? Omar Khayyám must have been similarly perplexed when he wrote the twenty-ninth stanza of the *Rubáiyát:* "Into this Universe, and Why not knowing/Nor Whence, like Water willy-nilly flowing;/And out of it, as Wind along the Waste,/I know not Whither, willy-nilly blowing."

In the last few decades, science has plunged headlong after many other long-standing philosophical problems. An old debate is the question of free will versus determinism in human actions. The Heisenberg uncertainty principle in physics, stating that the trajectories of individual particles cannot be predicted precisely, has provided welcome ammunition to the free will advocates, while the studies of genes, DNA, and the newborn field of sociobiology surely put glee in the hearts of the determinists. And then there's the ancient controversy about whether mind is distinct from matter. I imagine the mind-body problem has had to take stock of recent developments in neurobiology, especially the results indicating that specific mental activities like language and emotions may be localized to specific halves of the brain. Science has not really answered any of these questions, but continues to sharpen the focus.

And no matter how far it progresses, science generates more questions than it answers. Questions that disturb. Perhaps there is in science an inevitable incompleteness, analogous to that in mathematics proved by Kurt Gödel. Before Gödel's Proof, it was widely believed that each branch of mathematics, given sufficient axioms or rules of the game, was self-contained. In 1931 Gödel rigorously demonstrated that arithmetic contains true theorems that cannot be derived from the rules of arithmetic. In a similar manner I believe there may be meaningful questions about physical reality, the territory of science, whose study is intrinsically beyond the reach of any equations or experiments.

In all these mysteries we see ourselves. Would we be so intrigued if the human mind did not ponder why as well as how, if we did not have our Dalis and Sartres as well as our Madame Curies? This is surely another miracle, like the fragile balance of nuclear forces and the just-right release of the cosmic pendulum.

A Visit by Mr. Newton

One day last week I was sitting in my office at the Center for Astrophysics in Cambridge, tossing another irrelevant calculation into the wastebasket and praying to the Muses for some new ideas, when Isaac Newton walked in. I recognized him immediately from the pictures.

"How did you find the place?" I asked, a bit startled.

"Someone told me you were just south of the Holiday Inn on Mass Ave." Newton sat down, businesslike, in my extra chair. "Now, what can I do for you? My time is valuable. I've got a great little refresher course in optics, but it'll cost you."

I was in a complaining mood. "You guys had it easy. I can tell you, it's a lot harder to do scientific research these days. For one thing, every good idea I have, somebody's already thought of it. And the funding is in terrible shape. You can hardly get the necessary equipment. I wanted to buy my secretary a little word processor for typing and revising manuscripts, but the National Science Foundation won't fork over a cent.

"And who has time for research, anyway, when you have to keep current on all this," I groaned, pointing to stacks and stacks of unread journals piled up on my desk, on the floor, on the windowsill. "It must have been a joy to do science with less happening."

"What you need is another plague," Newton suggested. "I did some of my best work in 1665 and 1666, when the university was closed down and everybody was out sick."

Looking bored, Newton began snooping around my office, hesitated in front of the two stuffed and lacquered frogs playing dominoes that I had picked up in Acapulco, and finally settled in front of the bookcase. He started thumbing through the textbook on calculus and analytical geometry. "Damn. I thought I'd fixed Leibniz's wagon. I see he's still getting equal credit."

The telephone rang. It was Gruenwald at the University of Minnesota, whom I'd been trying to reach for days.

"There's another problem," I said, hanging up the phone. "How can you keep abreast of current developments when people never return your calls?"

I noticed that Newton was peering over some scribbled equations almost buried on the edge of my desk.

"What's this?" he asked.

"Oh, that. I'm investigating the electromagnetic radiation produced by a thin square sheet of gas in hyperbolic orbit around a neutron star."

"I see," said Newton, removing the sleeve of his robe from my coffee cup. "And what natural phenomena does your investigation explain?"

"Uh, it's a theoretical problem, of course. But my calculations should be a perfect test of the Ludwick-Friebald effect," I answered shrewdly. "A graduate student in Cincinnati is extremely interested in the result."

"Trifling. Hath not anything important in science transpired since my *Principia?*"

Newton was strict, but I would try to impress him. "Let's see. Darwin showed that species evolve by survival of the fittest. Einstein discovered that the flow of time is relative to the observer. De Broglie and Heisenberg and Schrödinger found that particles actually behave as waves and can be in several places at the same time. Watson and Crick discovered the structure containing the blueprint for reproducing life. We've developed very fast devices for mathematical computations, called computers, which are gradually taking over society. And about fifteen years ago men landed on the moon."

"Cheese?"

"No, sorry. I'm afraid that particular theory of yours didn't pan out. Oh, I almost forgot. A few years ago some guys invented a perpetual motion machine called supply-side economics."

Newton had that impatient look again, and I realized time was running out on a precious opportunity. All I wanted were a few profound ideas. To be honest, the Ludwick-Friebald effect was beginning to bore me. I'd just love to prance into the next meeting of the American

Physical Society with some brilliant new equations and show them I had the right stuff, after all.

Newton was flipping through my books again—differential equations, thermodynamics, quantum mechanics, radiation theory—muttering "trivial" after each book.

"Look, Mr. Newton," I said. "Here's a pad of paper and a pencil. I'd be grateful if you would write down some original results for me. Maybe something like a fourth law of motion. Or perhaps a new theory of elasticity."

Newton sat down at my desk, shoving aside the last ten issues of the *Astrophysical Journal,* and was silent for several minutes. "Well, I do have one item for you. I hate to admit it," he said sheepishly, "but I made a mistake in my universal law of gravitation. The force of gravity varies as the inverse cube of the distance, not the inverse square."

"You're kidding."

"No. I had to get it off my chest. You're the first person I've told."

This was big. In fact, this was so big maybe I should keep it secret for a while and milk it for all it was worth before announcing the news to my colleagues. Fernsworth at Princeton would be green with envy. Eventually NASA would certainly need to know. And the Pentagon, before the Russians found out. Come to think of it, this stuff would probably be classified the moment it leaked out.

"How did you realize you'd made a mistake?" I asked, after calming down.

"I could never account for this vicious left hook in my long wood shots, despite my best calculations and attempts to compensate. Finally, I decided the fundamentals had to be wrong, so I worked the problem backwards and

deduced the inverse cube law. I was too embarrassed to tell anybody at the time."

I gave a long, low whistle. This was even bigger than I thought. Palmer, Nicklaus. They could probably shave five strokes if they knew what I now knew. The implications of the inverse cube law were staggering.

"I want you to know," said Newton, "that I take no responsibility for the consequences. *Hypothesis non fingo.*"

"I understand." My mind was racing. Many things were beginning to fall into place. Mysterious phenomena that had always puzzled me now made perfect sense. Suddenly I could explain why Aunt Bertha always had trouble getting up from the dinner table. And why my folded pants always slid off the bedroom chair during the night. The more I thought about it, the logic of the inverse cube law seemed inescapable.

Newton was leaning back in his chair, exhausted. His eyes were glazed. I found myself warming up to the old boy since he had humbled himself in front of me. For the next half hour we talked of lighter subjects—some optics, a bit of kinetics, a little alchemy. Then he rose and, reciting a few lines from *Paradise Lost,* walked out of my office.

It has been a week now since Mr. Newton's visit. For the first few days I was paralyzed with the knowledge of the inverse cube law. Antigravity. Ketchup that pours instantly. New weapons of destruction. I could not sleep, I could not work.

Finally, I pulled myself together and nervously began to calculate. I bungled the first equation, wadded up the paper and lobbed it toward the garbage can, and began again. Out of the corner of my eye I noticed that the paper wad bounced off the blackboard, skidded along a file cabinet, knocked over one of the frogs from Acapulco, and landed cleanly in the can. Curious. That trajectory was exactly as predicted by Newton's original theory of gravity. I put down my pencil and threw another wad, then another, then another. Every shot confirmed the old inverse square law. I tipped over stacks of journals and clocked their motion, leaped repeatedly off my desk, hurled books across the room. Slowly, the stubborn truth began to dawn on me; Mr. Newton's original theory had always been right. I guess after all those centuries Newton had grown senile. They do say physicists peak at an early age.

Things have settled down, although my office is a mess. After a short vacation, I'm going back to the Ludwick-Friebald effect. It may not be important, but it's probably correct.

The Space Telescope

Sometime in 1986 the cargo bay of the space shuttle will open, three hundred miles above the Earth, and a mechanical arm will release into orbit a 42-foot-long cylinder containing a telescope. The Space Telescope, as it is called, has been twenty years in the planning and will cost the National Aeronautics and Space Administration and the European Space Agency nearly a billion dollars. It will dominate astronomical research for the rest of the century.

Why send a telescope into space? Because the Earth's atmosphere, while quite agreeable to most of us, is a headache to observational astronomers. First and foremost, the images of astronomical objects are blurred when light travels through the turbulent and clumpy air around the Earth: That's why stars twinkle. Beneath the murky atmosphere, ground-based optical telescopes cannot normally distinguish details separated in angle by less than about three ten-thousandths of a degree (the half sky has a total angle of 180 degrees). The Space Telescope will be able to see ten times more clearly than this—clearly enough, for example, to read the license plate of a car in Boston from as far away as Washington, D.C.

Ground-based telescopes also receive stray light from cities and from atmospheric auroras. Background light becomes confused with light from the object under study. Such unwanted contamination almost disappears high above the Earth's atmosphere. At visible wavelengths of light, outer space is about three times darker than earthly nights in most locations. With its decreased background light and increased angular resolving power, the Space Telescope will be able to see stars fifty times fainter than those observed by ground-based telescopes now in use.

Finally, atmospheric absorption prevents much of the telltale radiation produced by astronomical bodies from ever reaching Earth. This includes ultraviolet and infrared radiation, with wavelengths respectively shorter and longer than those of visible light. With appropriate instruments, the Space Telescope will gaze into several hundred times more of the electromagnetic spectrum than can comparable telescopes here on Earth.

Dreams of science in space are not new. More than a century ago, Jules Verne imagined exploration of Africa by balloon in his *Five Weeks in a Balloon*, published in 1863, and described manmade satellites in *From the Earth to the Moon* (1865). The German rocketry pioneer Hermann Julius Oberth was one of the first to point out that space is where telescopes ought to be. That was in 1923. The first astronomical observations in space were made in the late 1940s, using captured German V-2 rockets that were capable of poking above the atmosphere for a few minutes. In the late 1950s a U.S. telescope named Stratoscope I was lifted to the top of the atmosphere by balloon. The first orbiting astronomical satellites, with the precious advantages of stability and long lifetime, were operated by NASA in the 1960s.

In 1978 the United States placed two major astronomical satellites into orbit—the International Ultraviolet Explorer and the Einstein Observatory. The latter, at a cost of $200 million (in 1982 dollars), housed the first telescope able to focus X-rays, radiation of even shorter wavelength than the ultraviolet. Einstein ran out of gas in April 1981. More precisely, the small jets on the satellite, crucial for changing its orientation on command, ran out of gas. The Space Telescope, which will be serviced regularly by the space shuttle, should enjoy a lifetime of at least fifteen years. It is the next major scientific space project since Einstein.

As an illustration of the power of the telescope, consider its potential impact on several fundamental questions that keep astronomers up at night. One such question is whether there is any life in the universe beyond our own planet. At one time the chances of locating life forms on sister planets in our solar system seemed good. Unfortunately, the Viking landers that touched down on Mars found no signs of life. And Mars had been considered the best bet. What about planets circling stars other than the sun? There are one hundred billion stars just in our own galaxy, the Milky Way. Perhaps with the billions of possible temperatures, gravities, and chemical compositions on other worlds, life might flourish somewhere. But astronomers have not yet found a single example of another planetary system. Present ground-based telescopes simply cannot distinguish the relatively faint reflected light of a hypothetical planet from the much brighter light of its parent star, nor can they discern the tiny periodic wobble of the parent star in response to the gravity of an orbiting planet. Either of these phenomena would be a welcome tip-off. Of course finding other planetary systems in the universe isn't equivalent to documenting the footprints of extraterrestrials, but it may be an important first step.

For example, the star nearest the sun is Alpha Centauri, about 4.5 light-years distant. Alpha Centauri is not unlike our own sun. If it had a planetary system similar to our own, its position would not stay fixed but would shift back and forth by about a millionth of a degree. Ground-based telescopes are unable to detect such a small movement. The Space Telescope, however, should be able to sense the wobble of planet-bearing stars as far away as ten or twenty light-years and will be programmed to scrutinize a dozen or so candidates. Theoretical astronomers, who work only with pencil and paper, would be startled if space were not littered with planetary systems. Nevertheless, the question of our uniqueness seems sufficiently unsettling that it would be nice to know for sure.

How old is the universe? Since the 1920s we have known that the universe is in a state of expansion, with the galaxies rushing away from each other. If this moving picture is mentally played backward in time, then the galaxies crowd ever closer together until a definite instant in the past when all matter in the universe crushes together into a point of unimaginable density. Almost all astronomers and physicists accept the concept that the universe began with the Big Bang, when that matter started the expansion we still see. How long ago was it?

Since all galaxies originated from the same point in the Big Bang, the time elapsed since then is the time required for any galaxy some distance from the Milky Way to move to wherever it is now. Determining other galaxies' velocities and distances from our galaxy is therefore crucial. For example, if the galactic velocities were constant in time, a galaxy flying away at 0.1 billion light-years per year would take 10 billion years to put 1 billion light-years between itself and us. Astronomers have no trouble measuring the velocities of nearby galaxies to high accuracy, but their distances from us are presently known to only about 30 percent. In terms of the birthday of the universe, this translates to an uncertainty of several billion years.

Measuring cosmic distances is like climbing an endless ladder into space, where the size of each step is estimated by the height of the previous rung. To begin, you must somehow determine the distance to a nearby standard object, like a type G8 V star. All G8 V stars have the same intrinsic properties, including luminosity (absolute brightness). By comparing the *apparent* brightness of the type G8 V star with its distance from the observer, you can infer its luminosity. (The apparent brightness of a light source of given luminosity decreases as it moves farther away from the observer.) With G8 V stars in hand for calibration, you climb one rung up the ladder and seek out a G8 V star harbored within a brighter, more distant object—say a large globular cluster of stars. From the apparent brightness of the new G8 V star, whose luminosity was previously determined, you can judge the distance to the globular cluster; you can then calculate the luminosity of the cluster from *its* apparent brightness. In the process you have happily gained a new type of object for calibration, the globular cluster, and can now proceed onward up the ladder, perhaps looking for globular clusters embedded within galaxies. Needless to say, the higher you go up the ladder, the shakier it gets.

The first rung had better be very trustworthy. As Earth revolves around the sun and changes its perspective, the apparent positions of nearby stars shift on the night sky, providing an estimate of their distances (closer stars shift more). The Space Telescope, with its highly precise angular resolution, should be five times more accurate than ground-based telescopes in measuring the distances to nearby stars in this manner. For the next couple of rungs, taking us out to nearby galaxies, the Space Telescope should obtain improved measurements of certain stars used for calibration. Several rungs up the cosmic distance ladder and on solid footing, we may be able to determine the rate of expansion of the universe, and ultimately its age, to within several percent.

Do black holes exist? On paper, of course they do. However, aside from one strong candidate known as Cygnus X-1, about 7,000 light-years from Earth, astronomers have floundered in their search for these exotic objects. According to theory, black holes, which are collapsed stars, should have a very small size. (A black hole of the same mass as our sun would be 1.5 miles in diameter; larger black holes would have diameters in proportion to their mass.) There is a clever way of measuring such small sizes: All objects, on Earth or in space, are continually subject to disturbances, which produce variations in the emission of light and sound. In astronomy, the size of an object too distant to make out directly may be inferred from the rapidity of its light fluctuations, in much the same way that the size of a canyon can be estimated by the interval between echoes. An instrument aboard the Space Telescope will be able to distinguish light fluctuations spaced as closely as ten millionths of a second apart. Such a time interval would indicate an object whose size is ten millionths of a light second, or about two miles. Most black holes would be no smaller.

Another strategy for unmasking black holes is less direct. A massive black hole inhabiting the center of a galaxy, while busily chewing up stars, should force the surviving stars to huddle around it. The hapless stars queuing up for destruction should appear as a particular increase in light toward the center of the galaxy. So far this diagnostic effect has escaped detection by earthly telescopes. Again it is a matter of angular resolution. For galaxies within two million light-years of Earth, including Andromeda and several others, the Space Telescope should be able to peer within one light-year of the galactic center, perhaps close enough to see the handiwork of a black hole one hundred million times the mass of the sun.

To carry out its awesome business, the Space Telescope will require an impressive armament of on-board instruments, technical innovations, and organizational support on the ground. First, there is the telescope itself, which will have a 2.4-meter (94-inch) primary mirror to focus incoming light and is being built by the Perkin-Elmer Corporation. For analyzing the light, six scientific instruments are now scheduled to be on board the satellite: the wide-field/planetary camera, the faint-object camera, the faint-object spectrograph, the high-resolution spectrograph, the high-speed photometer, and the fine guidance system. Each is being built by a team of scientists and will have required more than eight years to complete by the time the telescope is launched.

A terrestrial photographer will be surprised not to find film in the Space Telescope. The two cameras record light intensities with fancy photoelectric cells known in the trade as CCDs (charge-coupled devices). Incoming light is broken up into its constituent colors by the two spectrographs, permitting such details as the temperatures and chemical compositions of objects in space to be deduced. The high-speed photometer measures the variability in the intensity of light and produces data that can be used, among other things, to infer the sizes of objects. Finally, the fine guidance system, with its gyroscopes and star identification systems, will hold the telescope's direction steady to three millionths of a degree over a period of ten hours, or a little more than six orbits.

Capitalizing on the technical opportunities in space has required breakthroughs in materials and design. A good example is the telescope's support structure, which holds the primary and secondary mirrors at a distance of 17 feet apart. Temperature changes in space could cause distortions in the structure, and expansion or contraction of as little as one ten-thousandth of an inch would produce tears in the data rooms on Earth. To solve the problem, Boeing Aerospace has developed for the structure a mixture of graphite, which expands with cold and contracts with heat, and epoxy, which expands with heat and contracts with cold.

Astoundingly, all this expensive hardware and technology is going to be shot off into space, largely unattended, and trusted. An on-board computer will control the program of observations. Communication with the telescope, including data retrieval, will occur via a pair of satellites, called the Tracking and Data Relay Satellite System (TDRSS), which are already hovering over fixed positions on the Earth's surface. On board, all data are digitized (converted into bits of information represented by ones and zeros) and can be stored on magnetic tape before radio transmission to the TDRSS satellites and then earthward to the Goddard Space Flight Center in Maryland— and human beings.

Observational astronomy these days, like many other fields of experimental science, has taken on a ghostly quality. It used to be that astronomers on "observing runs" would pack up several days of sandwiches and good books for the cloudy nights, travel to the top of a mountain somewhere, and sit at the eyepiece of a telescope, taking notes and photographs and simply enjoying the spectacle first hand. A colleague of mine, working with data from the Einstein satellite, recently completed a "hands-on" investigation of quasars. When I asked him what it was like, he allowed that in fact he had passed the time in front of a video screen just down the hall, pushing keys and pondering over various digitized images of the quasar from data stored on a magnetic tape. The information had previously been manipulated by two other computers, before which it had been retrieved from the TDRSS in space. It was irrelevant that the Einstein satellite, which alone "saw" the quasar, had been defunct for over a year. Digitized data keep well.

And there will be enormous quantities of data from the Space Telescope. To digest such an onslaught of cosmic information, a new facility, the Space Telescope

Science Institute, has recently been established on the campus of Johns Hopkins University. The institute, as well as the observing program of the telescope, will be administered for NASA by the Association of Universities for Research in Astronomy, a consortium of seventeen universities. The staff of the institute may eventually number 150 to 200 people, including 55 to 75 Ph.D.'s, comparable to or larger than the largest national facility now in operation for ground-based optical telescopes, Kitt Peak National Observatory in Tucson, Arizona. It is estimated that the yearly maintenance and operation cost of the telescope and the institute will be about $30 million—roughly the total capital cost of a state-of-the-art optical telescope on the ground and somewhat more than the yearly budget of Kitt Peak. An additional data center, at the European Southern Observatory in Munich, will be administered by the European Space Agency, which is contributing 15 percent of the cost of the telescope.

The Space Telescope represents an increasing trend in experimental science toward complex instruments, big bucks, and big management. Most scientists view this development as the natural consequence of merging new technology with science, a merger predicted by Francis Bacon long before the Industrial Revolution. The evolution toward big science is nowhere better illustrated than in the progress of telescopes, in which the Space Telescope stands as a crowning achievement. Telescopes were first applied to astronomy, beginning in 1610, by Galileo, who discovered mountains on the moon and moons around Jupiter. In 1982 dollars, Galileo's telescope (minus his signature) would cost about $100. While the ability to make bigger and smoother telescope lenses and mirrors steadily increased, new gadgets were developed for light analysis and operation. Spectrographs and photographs were invented in the 1800s, and photometers came into wide use in the 1930s. Modern computers bounded onto the stage with the invention of the vacuum tube in 1945, were made smaller and faster with the transistor in 1958, and became still smaller and faster with the silicon-chip integrated circuit in 1966.

Recent ground-based optical telescopes, like the 4-meter (157-inch) telescope at Kitt Peak, built in 1970, and the 4-meter Anglo-Australian Telescope, built in 1974, cost about $30 million each, again in 1982 dollars. The new Multiple Mirror Telescope in Mount Hopkins, Arizona, which has the novel design of six mirrors combined to produce one image with an equivalent mirror aperture of 4.5 meters, cost only $10 million. At a cost of about $800 million, the Space Telescope will be definitely out of sight.

A parallel trend has occurred in various areas of physics—for example, in the search for smaller and smaller structures. At close range the naked eye can distinguish structures a few thousandths of a centimeter in size, about the diameter of a human hair. The first microscope, constructed out of cardboard, wood, and vellum by Anton van Leeuwenhoek in the seventeenth century, brought bacteria into focus. It got down to sizes of less than one ten-thousandth of a centimeter, at a cost of about $100 in today's dollars. In recent searches for subnuclear structure, complexities and costs have soared. Dissecting matter, or whatever you call it at a millionth of a billionth of a centimeter, now requires the leviathan "particle accelerators," like Fermilab in Illinois, Brookhaven in New

York, and CERN in Switzerland. Fermilab, built in the late 1960s for several hundred million dollars, winds four miles around.

Other fields of basic, experimental science have not yet become consumed by such spectacular machines as the Space Telescope and the Fermilab accelerator, but they are drifting in that direction. None of this should quite surprise anyone. Scientists have grown accustomed to snooping around in territory far removed from human sense perception. As each science relies more and more on artificial eyes and ears, the snooping will cost more. And there may be something more. It seems we simply love machines. According to historian Lewis Mumford, our "technical narcissism" has been slowly building up steam for the last two thousand years.

An intriguing consequence of the mounting complexity and cost of doing science is that groups are replacing individuals. Although there are exceptions, the lone scientist sounding out nature in a personal lab, with home-made equipment, has become a dying breed. Says physicist Norman Ramsey of Harvard, "By and large, it's easier to invent a fundamental experiment that takes a big group. Otherwise, it would have been done already." Between the first five years (1958–1962) of the physics journal *Physical Review Letters* and the most recent five years, the average number of authors per experimental paper has increased from 4.6 to 7.0.

Furthermore, a healthy fraction of scientists are now working at large, federally funded national centers similar to the nascent Space Telescope Science Institute. These centers—the National Radio Astronomy Observatory in Charlottesville, Virginia, the NASA Goddard Space Flight

Center in Greenbelt, Maryland, the Los Alamos Scientific Laboratory, in New Mexico, and Brookhaven National Laboratory, to name a few—now include 55 percent of all astronomers and 45 percent of all physicists. Los Alamos alone has a staff of about a thousand physicists. To thrive in this kind of environment, the ambitious experimental scientist of today must be much more than a scientist. He or she must also be a manager, an organizer, a grant getter, an entrepreneur.

One wonders whether, in the caverns of big science, some of the bright youngsters might lose their way. Riccardo Giacconi, the new director of the Space Telescope Science Institute, believes that one should not place too much emphasis on the issue of depersonalization in modern science. "Although it is true that success requires a chain of command," he says, "it is not clear that most people should be doing independent research." But Giacconi adds: "On the other hand, I am worried whether you select against creativity and individuality by funding large projects."

Samuel Ting, professor of physics at MIT and winner of the 1976 Nobel Prize, agrees. "The trend toward big science is very unfortunate," he says. "Particularly in experimental particle physics, with its teams of thirty to three hundred people, a young physicist has an extraordinarily difficult time in showing himself. When I started twenty years ago, a particle physics experiment could still be done by four or five people. If I were to start again today, I would not go into this field."

Norman Ramsey says, "It's more fun to do things by yourself, without waiting for committee approval or government funding."

Ironically, the fundamental discoveries continue to be made by relatively small projects and small groups. In his book *Cosmic Discovery,* Martin Harwit, an astronomer at Cornell, concludes that none of the forty-three most important astronomical phenomena, including fourteen discovered since 1960, were originally identified at large national centers. In part, this simply reflects the greater time for the use of instruments allotted to individual scientists at private centers of research. The importance of independence and personalization is hard to quantify.

I will hazard the guess that many of the major discoveries of the Space Telescope will be made by small teams not directly associated with the Space Telescope Science Institute, perhaps not even looking for anything specific. Besides the regular investigations of the telescope, there is a wonderful category known as the serendipity mode, consisting of secondary observations made when observing time becomes unexpectedly available. For the big machines, just as for the human mind, discovery may hinge upon unscheduled operations.

Is the Earth Round
or Flat?

I propose that there are few of us who have personally verified that the Earth is round. The suggestive globe standing in the den or the Apollo photographs don't count. These are secondhand pieces of evidence that might be thrown out entirely in court. When you think about it, most of us simply believe what we hear. Round or flat, whatever. It's not a life-or-death matter, unless you happen to live near the edge.

A few years ago I suddenly realized, to my dismay, that I didn't know with certainty whether the Earth was round or flat. I have scientific colleagues, geodesists they are called, whose sole business is determining the detailed shape of the Earth by fitting mathematical formulae to *someone else's* measurements of the precise locations of test stations on the Earth's surface. And I don't think those people really know either.

Aristotle is the first person in recorded history to have given proof that the Earth is round. He used several different arguments, most likely because he wanted to convince others as well as himself. A lot of people believed everything Aristotle said for nineteen centuries.

His first proof was that the shadow of the Earth during a lunar eclipse is always curved, a segment of a circle. If the Earth were any shape but spherical, the shadow it casts, in some orientations, would not be circular. (That the normal phases of the moon are crescent-shaped reveals the moon is round.) I find this argument wonderfully appealing. It is simple and direct. What's more, an inquisitive and untrusting person can knock off the experiment alone, without special equipment. From any given spot on the Earth, a lunar eclipse can be seen about once a year. You simply have to look up on the right night and carefully observe what's happening. I've never done it.

Aristotle's second proof was that stars rise and set sooner for people in the east than in the west. If the Earth were flat from east to west, stars would rise as soon for occidentals as for orientals. With a little scribbling on a piece of paper, you can see that these observations imply a round Earth, regardless of whether it is the Earth that spins around or the stars that revolve around the Earth. Finally, northbound travelers observe previously invisible stars appearing above the northern horizon, showing the Earth is curved from north to south. Of course, you do have to accept the reports of a number of friends in different places or be willing to do some traveling.

Aristotle's last argument was purely theoretical and even philosophical. If the Earth had been formed from smaller pieces at some time in the past (or *could* have been so formed), its pieces would fall toward a common center, thus making a sphere. Furthermore, a sphere is clearly the most perfect solid shape. Interestingly, Aristotle placed as much emphasis on this last argument as on the first two. Those days, before the modern "scientific method," observational check wasn't required for investigating reality.

Assuming for the moment that the Earth is round, the first person who measured its circumference accurately was another Greek, Eratosthenes (276–195 B.C.). Eratosthenes noted that on the first day of summer, sunlight struck the bottom of a vertical well in Syene (modern Aswan), Egypt, indicating the sun was directly overhead. At the same time in Alexandria, 5,000 stadia distant, the sun made an angle with the vertical equal to $\frac{1}{50}$ of a circle. (A stadium equaled about a tenth of a mile.) Since the sun is so far away, its rays arrive almost in parallel. If you draw a circle with two radii extending from the center outward through the perimeter (where they become local verticals), you'll see that a sun ray coming in parallel to one of the radii (at Syene) makes an angle with the other (at Alexandria) equal to the angle between the two radii. Therefore Eratosthenes concluded that the full circumference of the Earth is 50 $\times$ 5,000 stadia, or about 25,000 miles. This calculation is within 1 percent of the best modern value.

For at least 600 years educated people have believed the Earth is round. At nearly any medieval university, the quadrivium was standard fare, consisting of arithmetic, geometry, music, and astronomy. The astronomy portion was based on the *Tractatus de Sphaera Mundi*, a popular textbook first published at Ferrara, Italy in 1472 and written by a thirteenth-century, Oxford-educated astronomer and mathematician, Johannes de Sacrobosco. The *Sphaera* proves its astronomical assertions, in part, by a set of dia-

grams with movable parts, a graphical demonstration of Aristotle's second method of proof. The round Earth, being the obvious center of the universe, provides a fixed pivot for the assembly. The cutout figures of the sun, the moon, and the stars revolve about the Earth.

By the year 1500, twenty-four editions of the *Sphaera* had appeared. There is no question that many people *believed* the Earth was round. I wonder how many *knew* this. You would think that Columbus and Magellan might have wanted to ascertain the facts for themselves before waving good-bye.

To protect my honor as a scientist, someone who is supposed to take nothing for granted, I set out with my wife on a sailing voyage in the Greek islands. I reasoned that at sea I would be able to calmly observe landmasses disappear over the curve of the Earth and thus convince myself, firsthand, that the Earth is round.

Greece seemed a particularly satisfying place to conduct my experiment. I could sense those great ancient thinkers looking on approvingly, and the layout of the place is perfect. Hydra rises about 2,000 feet above sea level. If the Earth has a radius of 4,000 miles, as they say, then Hydra should appear to sink down to the horizon from a distance of about 50 miles, somewhat less than the distance we were to sail from Hydra to Kea. The theory was sound and comfortable. At the very least, I thought, we would have a pleasant vacation.

As it turned out, that was all we got. Every single day was hazy. Islands faded from view at a distance of only eight miles, when the land was still a couple of degrees above the horizon. I learned how much water vapor was in the air but nothing about the curvature of the Earth.

I suspect that there are quite a few items we take on faith, even important things, even things we could verify without much trouble. Is the gas we exhale the same as the gas we inhale? (Do we indeed burn oxygen in our metabolism, as they say?) What is our blood made of? (Does it indeed have red and white "cells"?) These questions could be answered with a balloon, a candle, and a microscope.

When we finally do the experiment, we relish the knowledge. At one time or another, we have all learned something for ourselves, from the ground floor up, taking no one's word for it. There is a special satisfaction and joy in being able to tell somebody something you have pieced together from scratch, something you really know. I think that exhilaration is a big reason why people do science.

Someday soon, I'm going to catch the Earth's shadow in a lunar eclipse, or go to sea in clear air, and find out for sure if the Earth is round or flat. Actually, the Earth is reported to flatten at the poles, because it rotates. But that's another story.

Pas De Deux

In soft blue light, the ballerina glides across the stage and takes to the air, her toes touching Earth imperceptibly. *Sauté, batterie, sauté.* Legs cross and flutter, arms unfold into an open arch. The ballerina knows that the easiest way to ruin a good performance is to think too much about what her body is doing. Better to trust in the years of daily exercises, the muscles' own understanding of force and balance.

While she dances, Nature is playing its own part, flawlessly and with absolute reliability. On *pointe,* the ballerina's weight is precisely balanced by the push of floor against shoe, the molecules in contact squeezed just the right amount to counter force with equal force. Gravity balanced with electricity.

An invisible line runs from the center of the Earth through the ballerina's point of contact and upward. If her own center should drift a centimeter from this line, gravitational torques will topple her. She knows nothing of mechanics, but she can hover on her toes for minutes at a time, and her body is continuously making the tiny corrections that reveal an intimacy with torque and inertia.

Gravity has the elegant property that it accelerates everything equally. As a result, astronauts become weightless, orbiting Earth on exactly the same trajectories as their spaceships and thus seeming to float within. Einstein understood this better than anyone and described gravity with a theory more geometry than physics, more curves than forces. The ballerina, leaping upward lightly, hangs weightless for a moment amid flowers she has dropped midair, all falling on the same trajectory.

Now she prepares for a *pirouette,* right leg moving back to fourth position, pushing off one foot, arms coming in to speed the turn. Before losing balance she gets four rotations. Male dancers, on *demi-pointe* and with greater contact area, can sometimes go six or eight. The ballerina recovers well, giving her spin smoothly back to Earth and remembering to land in fifth position smiling. Briefly her feet come to rest, caught between the passage of spin and the friction of the floor. Friction is important. Every body persists in its state of rest or of uniform motion unless acted upon by outside forces. Every action requires a reaction.

The ballerina depends on the constancy of the laws of physics, even though she herself is slightly unpredictable. In this same performance last night she went only three and a half turns through her first *pirouette,* and then took the *arabesque* several feet from where she takes it now. Regardless of these discrepancies, the atoms in the floor, wherever she happens to touch and at one millisecond's notice, must be prepared to respond with faithful accuracy. Newton's laws, Coulomb's force, and the charge of electrons must be identical night after night—otherwise, the ballerina will misjudge the resiliency of the floor or the needed moment of inertia. Her art is more beautiful in its uncertainty. Nature's art comes in its certainty.

The ballerina assumes one pose after another, each fragile and symmetrical. In the physics of solids, crystal structures can be found that appear identical after rotations by one-half, one-third, one-quarter, and one-sixth of a circle. Crystals with one-fifth and one-seventh symmetries do not exist because space cannot be filled with touching pentagons or septagons. The ballerina reflects a series of natural forms. She is first ethereal, then lyrical. She has struggled for years to develop a personal style, embellished with fragments from the great dancers. As she dances, Nature, in the mirror, pursues its own style effortlessly. It is the ultimate in classic technique, unaltered since the universe began.

For an ending, the ballerina does a *demi-plié* and jumps two feet into the air. The Earth, balancing her momentum, responds with its own *sauté* and changes orbit by one ten-trillionth of an atom's width. No one notices, but it is exactly right.

Relativity for the Table

Whenever I go home to Memphis, the dinner conversation roams all over the place, just as when I was a child. My father still knows a great deal I don't, but nowadays he wants me to explain to him how I know the universe is expanding, or something similar. He is a gentle man, but he comes from a long line of businessmen, and he can tell when accounts don't add up.

Last visit, during dessert, he latched onto Einstein's theory of relativity. "I've been hearing all my life that Einstein had a new idea about time and space. Something about the flow of time being relative to who's measuring it. That bothers me. Suppose you and I have on identical Swiss wristwatches, and we synchronize them. Let's say it's two o'clock. And you drive out to Kroger's and back. Now why won't your watch still read exactly the same as mine? An hour is an hour."

Long after coffee, I got him to settle for an explanation of why two events that appear simultaneous to one person might not appear so to another, which, he agreed, had a lot to do with the relativity of time. By then it was bedtime, and we never finished. So this is for you, Dad— certainly not the most precise explanation of relativity, but one that makes sense to me, without equations.

I have to begin by saying that the relative nature of time and the other peculiar effects in Einstein's theory positively violate personal experience. That's because these effects wouldn't become noticeable to the human senses unless one went traveling at close to the speed of light, 186,000 miles per second. We can no better sense the consequences of relativity at our slow earthly speeds than we could see all the beautiful greens and blues and yellows if we were color-blind. Late nineteenth-century physicists, including Einstein, were also troubled by the failure of their intuition in coming to grips with relativity, so you're in good company. What this means is you'll have to put more faith than you're used to in supersensitive instruments and a trail of logical arguments, wherever it leads.

The crucial thing in relativity is that light has the same speed, regardless of who measures it. Now I'll explain what this means. Before understanding light, people knew all about sound. Sound needs a material to travel through, like air or water. When sound travels through a room, for example, the air molecules get pushed together, then pulled apart, then together again, and this back and forth motion works its way from one end of the room to the other. In fact, this traveling vibration of molecules *is* sound. When it reaches our ears, the vibrating air starts our eardrums vibrating and we say, "Aha, someone's calling."

Since sound involves the vibrations of a material medium, the speed of sound measured by someone will depend on the overall motion of that medium relative to the measurer. Let's say a friend calls you from a quarter mile away. If the wind is blowing toward you, you'll hear the call sooner than if the wind is blowing away from you. It's the same as a rowboat in a current. The rower maintains a constant speed relative to the water. Run along the river bank at the same rate and direction as the current and you'll see that speed. But stand still on the shore and you'll measure a faster speed if the boat's going downstream, a slower one if it's going upstream.

What's different about light is it doesn't need a material to carry it along. Light is a traveling vibration, like sound, but it's a vibration of pure energy rather than any material substance. This was first demonstrated to be the case in 1881 by the physicist Albert Michelson (who, for this work, was the first American to win the Nobel Prize, in 1907). Everyone naturally assumed that light traveled in some material medium, in which case its measured speed would vary with a change in the motion of the observer. To his astonishment, Michelson found the speed of light always exactly the same. As far as light is concerned, there's no such thing as moving with or against the wind, with or against the current. Independent of your own motion, or the motion of the source of light, you'll always see a light beam go by at 186,000 miles per second.

At first, this result may not seem all that strange, but consider this: From experience you know you'll get there sooner if you walk along instead of stand on a moving escalator. By walking, you add your speed to that of the escalator. Now suppose a light beam passes two women, one walking toward its source and one standing still. Common sense says the beam passes the moving person faster than the stationary one. But each woman would see the beam going by at the *same* speed. Our intuition about how motions should combine has tricked us.

Now, if you've digested all this, it's not hard to explain why two events that appear simultaneous to one person may not appear so to another. My favorite illustration is a version of one Einstein used himself. Imagine a train traveling through the countryside, and in one of the cars a person sets up a screen exactly in the center of the car and a light bulb at either end. The screen is wired so that if it is illuminated on both sides at precisely the same instant, a bell rings. Otherwise not. (Our traveler has brought along some fancy equipment.) The car is now darkened and the person arranges to turn on both light bulbs simultaneously. He can verify these two events happened simultaneously because the bell rings. Since the two light beams traveled the same distance to get to the screen, halfway down the car, and traveled with the same speed, they had to have been emitted from their bulbs at the same instant. Now let's analyze this experiment from my perspective, as I stand outside beside the tracks. I, of course, also hear the bell ring. The bell either rings or it doesn't, and a ringing bell undeniably signals that the two light beams struck the screen simultaneously. Prior to this, however, I observed the two light beams were emitted at different times, for the following reason: I saw one light beam traveling in the same direction as the train and one in the opposite direction. The first beam had to travel farther than half a car length before striking the screen, because during its time of transit the train moved forward a bit. By the same token, the second beam traveled less. Since both beams have the same speed for me as well as for the man in the train (remember, the speed of light is independent of the motion of the source or observer!), the first beam had to have been emitted slightly before the second. For ordinary train speeds and lengths, this delay would be something like one hundredth of one trillionth of a second—hardly noticeable, but detectable by highly precise clocks. While clocks in the train would show the two light beams traveled precisely the same length of time, clocks on the ground would not. What were simultaneous events to the man in the train happened at different times for me.

As you would guess, these kinds of discrepancies get bigger as the relative velocity between the two observers increases. If the train were not moving at all relative to me, the fellow on the train and I would agree exactly on everything having to do with time. At the other extreme, if the train were moving by me at almost the speed of light, the first beam would travel a great distance before overtaking the screen and the other beam practically not at all, so that the two events of emission, from my frame of reference, would be widely separated in time.

You might at this point be willing to admit that odd things happen when light is specially involved, but otherwise prefer to stick with your common sense. However, in my train illustration light served only as a convenient tool for measuring time. The emission of light at the two ends of a train car could be the herald of *any* two events in those locations—the birth of two babies, for example, in which case different observers would disagree on whether they were born at the same time. Constancy of the speed of light has far-reaching implications. Pushing these implications to the end of the line, and against all common sense—like the Greeks who suggested the sun did not orbit the Earth—Einstein showed how time intervals in general depend on the motion of the people and clocks doing the measuring. The passage of time is not absolute, as it seems. And that's the gist of relativity.

Students and Teachers

In the fall of 1934, one year after his Ph.D., John Archibald Wheeler traveled to Copenhagen to study with the great atomic physicist Niels Bohr. At his Institute for Theoretical Physics, a house-sized building on Blegdamsvej 15, Bohr had created a scientific "school" in which the daily stimulation from brilliant seminars and disturbing new ideas could dismast slow thinkers. Among the students who had held up well were Felix Bloch, Max Delbrück, Linus Pauling, and Harold Urey, all future Nobel Prize winners like their teacher. As Wheeler arrived at the institute on bicycle one morning, he noticed a workman tearing down the vines that had grown thickly over the gray stucco front. On closer view, he saw it was Bohr himself, "following his usual modest but direct approach to a problem." Thus began Wheeler's tutelage.

I am, through Wheeler, a great grandstudent of Bohr. I had forgotten this fact until a recent venture to the Boston studio of painter Paul Ingbretson, who immediately announced his own pedagogical descent from R. H. Ives Gammell, a student of William Paxton, a student of the academic painter Jean-Léon Gérôme. In the art world it is commonly said that the days of the master and apprentice tradition ended two centuries ago, that the classical method of severe and thorough training has been lost, except by a handful of painters. Ingbretson, 34 years old, is one of that handful. He treasures the technique and style and wisdom garnered from his teachers and tries to give away some of it to his pupils here in the Fenway Studios, where Paxton worked from 1905 to 1914. What he learned from Gammell and Paxton cannot be written down. He is a living painting, full of their brush strokes and visions. In science, such personal inheritance receives less currency, following the idea that a cut-and-dried objectivity outlives questions of style. You rarely witness a scientist exhibiting his pedagogical lineage. Yet without a good teacher, a young student of science could read a row of textbooks stretching to the moon and not learn how to practice the trade. Exactly what is it, in this age of massive information storage and retrieval, that you can't learn from a book?

"Squint your eyes; squint your eyes," Ingbretson was admonishing one of his students. By squinting the eyes as you study your subject, minor details fade, leaving only the highlights, the dominant lights and darks. Ingbretson's charges, with their easels and paper and charcoal, were clustered around a classical marble bust, lit from windows rising to the 16-foot ceiling of the studio. "It's all a question of learning to see," Ingbretson was saying. This phrase "learning to see" was one Gammell often used. It typifies the method of painting from nature practiced by

the early twentieth-century Boston school, the blend of the exacting academic style with impressionism.

Wheeler, now 72, had his own method of learning how to see, which he taught to my teacher Kip Thorne: "If you're having trouble thinking clearly, imagine programming a computer to solve your problem. After mentally automating the necessary logic, step by step, you can then dispense with the computer." On occasion, marching through a problem in such a fashion will lead to an unexpected contradiction, and this is where the fun really begins. Wheeler loves to teach physics in terms of paradoxes, a habit he picked up from Bohr. In the 1920s and 1930s—when quantum mechanics was in its infancy and physicists were slowly adjusting to the strange fact that an electron behaves both as a localizable particle and as a wave, spread over many places at once—Bohr realized that several apparently conflicting views can be equally essential for understanding some phenomena. A student doesn't get this kind of thinking from books. Wheeler recalls Bohr's usual method of explanation as a one-man tennis match, in which each hit of the ball would be some telling contradiction to previous results, raised by a new experiment or theory. After each hit Bohr would run around to the other side of the court quickly enough to return his own shot. "No progress without a paradox." The worst thing that could happen in a visitor's seminar was the absence of surprises, after which Bohr had to utter those dreaded words, "That was interesting."

I was slowly circling an odd still-life arrangement in the clutter of Ingbretson's studio—an upright porcelain plate with a diagonal pattern, a bowl, a matchbox, a bit of dried flowers. On an easel nearby was an extremely effective rendering by one of Ingbretson's advanced pupils, clearly taken from the pale still life in front of me, yet more interesting somehow. Then I slipped around to the precise viewing angle of the drawing and suddenly the objects on the table leaped out at me in a wonderful way. "Some artists," said Ingbretson, "will arrange and rearrange a still life for hours until they find just the right grouping and viewing angle." You look at it from the wrong direction and all you've got is a collection of junk. "Sometimes reality isn't enough. I was once doing a still life in Gammell's class, and we had meticulously chosen and arranged the objects beforehand. After I was finished Gammell stared at my work for a few minutes and then told me to draw in a nonexistent knicknack in the corner. It turned out he was right."

Graduate students in science, unanchored to a knowledgeable thesis adviser, have wasted years circling around for a good project. Every so often an application comes in from a Third World student wanting a research position abroad, and you can tell he's highly competent mathematically and he's been combing the journals equation by equation, but his teachers are isolated from mainstream research, and he has no clue as to what projects are worth working on. The Nobel-Prize-winning Soviet physicist Lev Landau kept a notebook of about thirty important unsolved problems, which he would show to students if and when they successfully passed a barrage of tests known affectionately as the Landau Minimum. Significant research projects in science are often no more difficult than insignificant ones. Projects out of Landau's notebook had guaranteed significance.

As a student, you could always tell which projects Thorne was hot on, because the hallway near his office was lined with framed wagers between himself and other scientific eminences. "Kip Steven Thorne wagers S. Chandrasekhar that rotating black holes will prove to be stable. K. S. T. places forward a year's subscription to *The Listener;* S. C. places forward a year's subscription to *Playboy.*" And so on. Thorne, red-bearded and wiry, would sit quietly in his office filling pages with equations, while passing students contemplated those wagers in the hall and were set on fire.

Beethoven and Czerny and Liszt, Socrates and Plato and Aristotle, Verrocchio and Leonardo, Pushkin and Baryshnikov. As we stood in the studio, Ingbretson walked over to a pupil who had succeeded in putting down three questionable lines in the last hour and told her to start from scratch. Ingbretson's own teacher demanded a lot from his students and didn't mind a little humiliation to get a point across. One day while a younger Ingbretson was smugly reflecting on his painting, Gammell, a bald, wizened man with the head of a bulldog, standing not much over five feet, took Ingbretson by his pinky, led him around the room to some white paint, dipped the little finger in the paint, then led him back to the canvas and applied the finger to a strategic spot. "There," said Gammell, "now you've got the highlight." Hans Krebs, winner of the 1953 Nobel Prize in medicine or physiology, a student of Nobelist Otto Warburg, a student of Nobelist Emil Fischer, wrote that scientists of distinction, above all, "teach a high standard of research. We measure everything, including ourselves, by comparisons; and in the absence of someone with outstanding ability there is a risk that we easily come to believe we are excellent.... Mediocre people may appear big to themselves (and to others) if they are surrounded by small circumstances. By the same token big people feel dwarfed in the company of giants, and this is a most useful feeling.... If I ask myself how it came about that one day I found myself in Stockholm, I have not the slightest doubt that I owe this good fortune to the circumstance that I had an outstanding teacher at the critical stage of my scientific career."

Rulers and plumb bobs appear regularly in Ingbretson's studio. A plumb bob is a weight attached to a string and, when freely hung in the earth's gravitational pull, gives an unerring reading of the vertical direction. Rulers and plumb bobs serve as invaluable tools for getting proportion and angles exactly right. This old tradition of expert draftsmanship was gleaned from Gammell, who learned it from Paxton. Paxton's portraits are stunning in their precision, with a reality and sensuality far exceeding any photograph. Of Paxton, Gammell once wrote "His unsurpassed visual acuity combined with great technical command enabled him to report his impressions with astounding veracity."

One of Ingbretson's students was struggling with angles in her drawing of the marble bust. Lines were going awry and wandering aimlessly. The sacred plumb bob wasn't working. "Aha," he offered, "your paper's gotten tilted."

Learning good draftsmanship requires constant feedback between teacher and student, Ingbretson explained. But good draftsmanship isn't enough. After mastering technique, you then must decide what to emphasize on the canvas. This tricky combination of formal method and individual impression has the flavor of the balance between mathematical rigor and physical intuition required in science. Thorne believes a feeling for such balance is one of the crucial things he learned from Wheeler. "Many scientists move at a snail's pace because they are too mathematical and don't know how to think physically. And vice versa for people too sloppy in their mathematics." Consider, for example, a quantitative description of marbles rolling around on a floor with holes in it. You try to derive an equation that tells how the number of marbles decreases in time. A most useful check of that equation is to set the hole size to a small number, which should yield the result that you don't lose any of your marbles. Or else the equation is wrong. This check wouldn't naturally occur to you unless you have a physical picture in your head of marbles rolling around and falling, one by one, through the holes. The mathematical equation itself, right or wrong, is quite content to stare back with an unrevealing jumble of its marble-conserving and marble-nonconserving parts.

Niels Bohr was a barrel-chested man, a football hero in his younger days. He was also gentle, and made his penetrating points in a soft voice. Bohr had many ideas he never tried to copyright. Likewise, his student John Wheeler, who quietly introduced numerous seminal ideas in physics, who performed an important but little-known role advising the Du Pont company during the Manhattan Project. Personal style can be inherited. Wheeler's student, Kip Thorne, has always bent over backward to give credit to other scientists. He begins seminars by attributing most of his results to particular students. Modesty, and its opposite, set the tone of a research group.

Ghirlandajo and Michelangelo, Koussevitsky and Bernstein, Lastman and Rembrandt, Fermi and Bethe, Luria and Watson. Of the 286 Nobel laureates named between 1901 and 1972, 41 percent had a master or senior collaborator who was also a Nobelist. Many Nobelists have surrounded themselves with spirited schools of students. A cluster of apprentices seems to generate, en masse, the necessary speed for takeoff. Among the great recent masters in physics were Thomson and Rutherford in England, Landau and Zel'dovich in the Soviet Union, Bohr in Denmark, Fermi and Oppenheimer and Alvarez in the United States—all with large research groups that spawned other eminent scientists. At Caltech, Thorne has always insisted on cloistering his half dozen students within adjacent rooms, with an unwritten rule that office and lab doors remain open. Someone, in a group of creative people working together, is usually quivering at the edge of discovery, and the vibrations spread.

Gazing out from a photograph of the Boston Museum's 1913 life-drawing class is a mustached, steady-eyed Paxton, sitting among his seventeen students. On the front left is Gammell, twenty years old, wearing an overcoat and a full head of hair. His expression is serious. The other pupils stand or sit, some wear elegant suits and others short sleeves and smocks, some look frightened and others bored, but they lean into each other with hands on shoulders, and there is electricity in the air.

The light was fading from the tall windows in Ingbretson's studio and his pupils were packing up their materials. "You know, Gammell wasn't perfect. His gestures were forced. Look at that arm." Ingbretson held up an illustration in a book of Gammell's paintings. "That's unnatural. It took me a while to see it. I was relieved."

Nothing is more bracing for students than to discover the fallibility of their exalted teachers. Students, God knows, are brimming with their own human weaknesses, and if their great mentors can make mistakes, well then, anything might happen. Thorne remembers that, during his second year of graduate school, Wheeler stuck by some erroneous statements about black holes. The realization of Wheeler's errors provided its own kind of inspiration. When Wheeler was in Copenhagen in 1934, he sought Bohr's assessment of some calculations on the so-called dispersion theory, extending it from applications where particles move slowly to applications where they move at nearly the speed of light. Bohr was skeptical of Wheeler's work and discouraged publication. Bohr was wrong. Perhaps, in the end, our own imperfection is the most vital thing we learn from teachers. At the dedication of the giant statue of Einstein in Washington a few years ago, Wheeler said "How can we best symbolize that science reaches after the eternal? . . . Not by a pompous figure on a pedestal. No, a figure over which children can crawl. . . ."

If Birds Can Fly,
Why Oh Why Can't I?

Human physical capacity is greatly restricted by natural laws, nowhere better illustrated than by our inability, despite vigorous and patient flapping of the arms, to fly. But the problem here is not simply the lack of wings. Scale up a pheasant to the size of a man and it would plummet to earth like a rock. Or consider Icarus. In the very plausible picture of him in my childhood mythology book, each attached wing equals his height and is about one quarter as wide—not unlike the graceful proportions of a swallow. Unfortunately, to fly with those wings the boy would have to beat his arms at one and a half horsepower, four times the maximum sustained output of an athletic human being. Icarus and Daedalus may have been willing to utterly exhaust themselves in their aerial escape from Crete, but most of us would like to go with better equipment.

Weight, shape, and available power all play a part in the science of flying. Let us begin with the most obvious requirement to fly: a lifting force must counterbalance the weight of the animal in question. That lift is provided by air. Air has weight and, at sea level, pushes equally in all directions with a pressure just under 15 pounds per square inch of surface. To achieve lift, an animal must manage to reduce the air pressure on its top surface, thereby creating a net pressure pushing upward from below. Birds and airplanes do this with properly formed wings and forward motion. The curvature and trailing edge of a wing force the air to flow more rapidly over its top side than its bottom. This causes a net upward pressure in proportion to the air density and to the square of the forward speed, a basic law of physics deriving from the conservation of energy. Thus with every doubling of the speed comes a quadrupling of the lift pressure. No motion, no net lift pressure. Likewise, birds couldn't fly on the moon, where the air density is essentially zero. (Under the moon's reduced gravity, however, creatures could jump six times as high as on Earth, which might be a happy substitute.)

Once you've got your lift pressure of so many pounds per square inch, you want to have out as many square inches of wing as practical. For example, a lift pressure of a hundredth pound per square inch (obtained by flying at about 35 miles per hour) pushing on a wing area of 400 square inches will yield a total lift force of 4 pounds, enough to buoy the weight of the average bird. There is a convenient tradeoff here: the necessary lift force can be had with less wing area if the animal increases its forward speed, and vice versa. Birds capitalize on this option according to their individual needs. The great blue heron, for example, has long, slender legs for wading and

must fly slowly in order not to break them on landing. Consequently, herons have a relatively large wing span. Pheasants, on the other hand, maneuver in underbrush and would find large wings cumbersome. To remain airborne with their relatively short and stubby wings, pheasants fly fast. Illustrating with some actual numbers, which I got by telephone from a helpful man at the Audubon Society who happened to have the birds in his office, an average great blue heron weighs in at six and a half pounds and projects a wing area of about 800 square inches, while a typical pheasant has three times the weight to wing area. However, the pheasant flies at a brisk 50 miles per hour, twice the speed of the heron.

How a bird propels itself forward, without propellers, is not obvious. This mystery was clarified in the early nineteenth century by Sir George Cayley, father of the modern airplane. (Leonardo Da Vinci spent years studying the art of flying and may well have understood the propulsion of birds, but his notes went undiscovered until a hundred years ago and, as typical, were left unfinished—although he did, as legend has it, launch one of his pupils from Mount Cecere in a flying contraption, which promptly crashed.) Birds, in fact, do have propellers, in the form of specially designed feathers in the outer halves of their wings. These feathers, called primaries, change their shape and position during a wing beat. On the downstroke they move downward and forward; on the upstroke, upward and backward. The primary feathers, operating on the same physical principles as the rest of the wing, produce their lift in the forward rather than upward direction.

Flying, like other physical activities, costs energy. A frictionless bird, having attained level flight and satisfied with its course, could glide forever, without moving a muscle. All the flapping, and expense of energy, is made necessary by air drag. Depending on a craft's aerodynamic design, the drag force is something like a twentieth of the lift force. To counteract drag, a cruising heron must pay out energy at the grudging rate of a fiftieth of a horsepower, leaving behind its calories in the form of stirred up pockets of air. Heavier birds of the same proportions have to use even more power for each pound of weight. Quadruple a bird's dimensions in every direction, keeping the shape identical, and its weight and volume increase by 64 times, while the power required to fly is 128 times larger. The only way around this law is to change shape. For example, if you hold the total volume (and weight) fixed, but increase the wing area four times, you can fly with half the power. For the long flights in migration, birds save power by flying together in formation, each member in the rear partially boosted by the rising air current trailing the next bird up and taking turns in the lead positions. But for solo flight, weight and shape inescapably determine the power needed to fly. These are the facts of life for aviation.

We now turn to biology, where we find that, pound for pound, living creatures are highly inefficient at producing useful power compared to internal combustion engines. A human being can maintain a maximum mechanical power output of only about one two-hundredth that of an engine of the same weight. For biology to reach twelve horsepower, the output of the little engine on the

Wright brothers' 1903 airplane, requires the services of an elephant.

The predicament of limited biological power lessens, however, as we proceed to smaller and smaller size. Lighter animals have more power for each pound of weight than heavier ones. Begin with a 450-pound horse, which has at its disposal one horsepower. Now reduce the weight of the animal. For every 50 percent reduction of weight, it is found that the power available for work diminishes by only 40 percent. By the time you're down to less than an ounce, you realize the 4,000 mice that weigh the same as a man have nine times the total power. Embarrassing perhaps, but not unexpected. Unlike most engines and machines, the muscles in animals generate more heat than useful work. Since heat production cannot be sustained at a greater rate than the animal can cool, and cooling is generally accomplished via the skin surface, animals will produce heat, and mechanical power, approximately in proportion to their surface area. The ratio of power output to weight, therefore, is close to the ratio of surface area to volume. It is then simple mathematics that smaller objects have greater surface area to volume than larger ones. Very small animals do have their own drawbacks, like the obligation to eat for most of the day, but that's another story.

Now, as the power needed to fly increases more rapidly with increasing weight than the power generally available—unless some spectacular change in body shape is effected—lightweight creatures clearly have the edge for flying. Nature seems quite appreciative of this struggle between physics and biology. Although birds have been experimenting with flight for 100 million years, the heaviest true flying bird, the great bustard, rarely exceeds 32 pounds. The larger, gliding birds such as vultures, lifted by rising hot air columns, do not carry their full weight. The 300-pound ostrich never leaves the ground, apparently having chosen sheer bulk rather than flight for defense.

Never having seen a 200-pound bird aloft, the British industrialist Henry Kremer must have felt his money safe for a long time when in 1959 he offered a prize of £5,000 for human-powered flight. In 1973, after many serious but unsuccessful attempts by Britain, Japan, Austria, and Germany, the Kremer prize was increased to the equivalent of $86,000. According to the strict rules of the offer, as set up by the Royal Aeronautical Society of England, a winning flight would have to traverse a figure eight around two pylons half a mile apart, never touching earth, and cross the start and finish point at least 10 feet above the ground. And, of course, the human pilot would have to furnish the power.

On August 23, 1977, in Shafter, California, an athletic young man climbed into a fragile, ungainly craft named the Gossamer Condor, strapped his feet to a pair of bicyclelike pedals connected to a propeller, and captured the prize. The flight lasted about seven and a half minutes.

What Paul MacCready, the designer of the craft, had done was to create an extraordinarily lightweight structure of enormous wing span. To keep the wing as light as possible, it was fashioned from mylar stretched over aluminum struts, with piano wire for bracing and cardboard for the wing's leading edge. The entire craft, including fuselage and wing, weighs 70 pounds. To this you have to add the weight of Bryan Allen, 135 pounds. Allen is approximately 6 feet tall; his wing was 96 feet long and 10 feet wide. Never has Mother Nature conceived a flying creature remotely approaching such disproportions. For numerical comparison, the pheasant has a wing area per mean body area of just over 1, the heron has 5, and the great bustard has 13. The Gossamer Condor (with pilot) has a wing area per mean body area of 90.

In many ways, human beings circumvented the difficulties of aviation long ago, at Kitty Hawk. And internal combustion engines date back even earlier. But in our dreams, when we soar into the air to escape danger or to simply bask in our strength, we fly as birds, self-propelled. It may be awkward to imagine ourselves installed with 100 feet of wing, but that's what Nature asks, to fly like a bird.

Cosmic
Natural Selection?

If you walk around Cambridge on a sultry summer night, you can hear a breathy hum come in and fade out as you pass each apartment, the sounds of the air conditioners. Every one of these splendid machines is surging with 1,000 or 2,000 watts of power, generated by Cambridge Electric Light Company. Nowadays, the vagaries of the local weather don't seem much of a bother. We can pipe water hundreds of miles to make deserts bloom, and we can pipe electricity across town to keep cool on a summer night.

Several miles away, at Massachusetts General Hospital, a 30-year-old man with a massive coronary attack has just been brought in. Within precious minutes a catheter is threaded through the femoral artery, up to the aorta below his heart. Sensors monitor the electrical activity of the heart muscle. As each expansion or contraction is anticipated, a small balloon attached to the end of the catheter alternately inflates and deflates, acting, in effect, as a secondary heart. With modern medicine and technology we human beings can survive major organ failures that would drop other animals dead in their tracks. And our success is much broader than state-of-the-art techniques in emergency rooms. Since about 1850, with the advent of immunizations and public health programs, the life expectancy in developed countries has dramatically increased from 40 to 75 years. The weaknesses of our bodies are no longer mysteries that we must live or die with, without putting up a good fight.

It may not be nice to fool Mother Nature, but that's what we're doing. By most counts, we seem to have bypassed the normal evolutionary forces that, over several billion years, distilled and refined Homo sapiens from the blue-green algae. What meaning has the concept of survival of the fittest, when applied to a society that irrigates deserts and shapes glass to correct the vision of its members? Alfred Russel Wallace, codiscoverer of natural selection, noted over a century ago that while animals evolve by means of adapting themselves to their environment, humans evolve by adapting the environment to themselves.

Some modern geneticists and biologists refer to the qualitative change in the development of our species as a transition from organic to sociocultural evolution. This transition has been associated with the emergence of agriculture, writing, printing, and even television—all the means at our disposal for passing along knowledge and culture. In contrast, organic evolution depends on physiologic structure and changes, the long-term stability but occasional alterations of particular nucleotides in DNA molecules. Nothing more clearly shows our break from biologic tradition than that we now manufacture genes in the laboratory, altering the game plan of bacteria to our own design. As a species, we have grown up and are moving out of the house.

What we are moving into is an environment created by our own intellectual activity and changing faster than we can keep up. In 1973, when I was a graduate student, the electronic pocket calculators burst into the market, the result of advances in computer miniaturization. My first calculator, a Hewlett-Packard 45, could whisk through exponentiations and inverse tangents at the push of a button and was smaller than a paperback novel. I promptly put my slide rule out to pasture. Only five years later I bought a Texas Instruments 59, which for half the price could do everything the old calculator did and was programmable as well. The old Hewlett-Packard now lies in a drawer somewhere collecting dust, a Model T of the computer industry.

It was less than forty years between Maxwell's equations of electromagnetism and the invention of radio, less than seventy years between the first flight of the Wright brothers and landing a man on the moon, less than thirty years between Watson and Crick's discovery of the structure of DNA and the adoption of recombinant DNA techniques to produce insulin. This is the setting that is molding our evolution, and it is itself changing shape not over millions of years or even tens of thousands of years, but over a single human lifetime. Technologically speaking, it is impossible to keep in style.

Where is all this leading? Will our brains eventually be linked to computers, providing each of us with an enormous and instant library of information? Will our retinas be reengineered to detect infrared and X-rays, as well as light at the "visible" frequencies? Would these changes affect personal communication or alter the family unit? In Isaac Asimov's classic 1950s science fiction series, *The Foundation* trilogy, social science has been perfected along with technology to such a degree that the experts can make accurate, long-term social and technological forecasts, predicting specific trends over many thousands of years. I do not believe that we will ever have the ability to make such evolutionary predictions. There are too many variables and the interconnections are too pervasive. We are continuously creating the environment and it is creating us. And it is all happening at blazing speed.

Still, we cannot afford to steer blindly. There probably are *some* principles of natural selection quietly at work, hidden beneath all the excitement. It has been suggested that the key to successful evolution in most species is an increasing diversification and complexity of organization—an idea more general than the organic or socio-cultural distinction. Perhaps our society should avoid becoming too monolithic, should attempt to preserve cultural and social differences. Most likely, we also need some new frontiers, where we can unwind and stretch out a bit.

Space exploration and development may be just the thing. Space offers endless opportunities for diversity and fresh challenges, and will pull us away from the danger of contemplating our navels on Earth. In space we will be children again. We have already made a small beginning with our communications satellites and probe vehicles to nearby planets. But far more awaits us.

Just in the last decade there have been a number of practical studies, by physicist Gerard O'Neill and others, of the possibilities of industrializing and colonizing the solar system. It has been estimated that by the year 2000 a self-sufficient colony of 10,000 people could be sustained in each of many giant rotating cylinders in space. By the year 2010, according to these studies, much of Earth's energy requirements could be satisfied by satellites that beam down solar energy in the form of microwave radiation, much of our mineral requirements satisfied by mining the moon and asteroids. It is not surprising that the estimated time frame for these developments is twenty to thirty years—that is roughly the same time frame for almost every item in the current technology explosion. These are not the romantic speculations of Jules Verne, but honest attempts to size things up on a dollars and cents basis. Physicist and visionary Freeman Dyson has argued that space colonization pursued in the style of the Mayflower expedition of 1620, rather than the costly Apollo program of the 1960s, could be done at a reasonable cost. Indeed, in the near future space development may hinge more on political and social issues than on economic ones.

When you also consider the dwindling resources on Earth, the increasing pollution of the biosphere, and the frighteningly real possibility of blowing ourselves off the planet any day, space seems even more appealing. We may have something less than a century to become independent of the limitations of our planet. Assuming this comes off well, there will be plenty of growing room. It has been estimated that in several thousand years we could fully develop the solar system, and perhaps tap a large fraction of the energy output of our central star, the sun. By that time, we may also be contemplating scout parties to nearby stars. In the long run, we will have to continually branch out, keeping ahead of the boundaries and problems we leave behind.

If we are very successful, our descendants may live to make contact with an extraterrestrial intelligence. In all the calculations that are done on the probability of such contact, a principal uncertainty is the lifetime of a technological civilization. Longer-lived cosmic societies have a greater chance of appropriately overlapping with each other in time. In these terms our own civilization is in its technological infancy, born about eighty years ago with the first radio broadcasts.

Taking a grand view of things, perhaps a principle of "cosmic natural selection" operates among the advanced forms of life in the universe. Societies that can manage to stay on top of their technologies and get into space while the getting's good survive a long time, maybe long enough to share their Chopin and Rembrandts and quantum mechanics with similar farsighted societies. And if we Earthlings are the only advanced life in the universe, then the burden to preserve that life is even greater. The blue-green algae would be proud.

Mirage

In southeast Persia lies the city Khashabriz. Few inhabitants have ever left its borders, for it is imprisoned within an outer city, a circle of castles and pilasters rising from the horizon like a mountain range. At times, aqueducts and windows glitter in the distance, but then dissolve. Some have ventured toward that outer fortress, only to find the castles receding in step, discouraging further exploration. It is said that, in time, a resident of Khashabriz grows resigned to confinement, walking the same cobblestone streets, passing the same food stalls filled with dates and wheat and sugar beets, breathing the same dusty air, marrying his children to the children of neighbors. When caravans and nomads sometimes drift into the city, they remain.

Like Zarathustra, the city has slowly wrapped around itself, content with isolation. No cotton in the outside world could be as silky as the cotton in Khashabriz, no pottery as delicate, no poets as enchanting. Indeed, what reason could there be to leave?

Over the years, various theories have developed among the citizens of Khashabriz regarding the origin of the distant, misty towers. One theory holds they were built by the ancient founders, to give protection from the unknown world beyond. Another claims they were erected as a blockade by foreign artisans, fearing competition with the curious silverwork and stunning carpets made within the inner city. The number of theories equals the number of people who discuss them idly in the vaulted alleys of the bazaars and on the terraces in late afternoon. On one point there is agreement: None dwell in that outer fortress because at night, while in Khashabriz the taverns and the houses glow with light, out there it is as black as coal. Except in sleep. Long ago it was discovered that the towers loom in every dream of every citizen of Khashabriz, just as in daylight they hover in the background beyond every shop, every house, every arcade.

A small group of local scientists, known for their detachment, have proposed that the surrounding castles are simply a mirage, that the people could escape at any time. They say that irregularities in the atmosphere cause light rays to bend, that the air can act as a misshapen lens, distorting some images and creating others. Similar effects, they say, disjoint the image of a spoon half in air and half in water. Most of their theorizing takes place in a little café after the evening meal and would occupy the whole of the night if their families did not call them home to sleep.

Their theory hinges on one peculiar fact: if the air density decreases with height above the ground, as hap-

pens when the temperature increases, light will bend down along its path and images will shift upward. An observer, recreating reality by extrapolating from the light rays striking his eyes, has the impression of being inside a large bowl and sees the image of the ground curving up into a distant wall. What's more, elaborate layerings of the atmosphere can fashion turrets where there was smoothness, stripes where there was solid gray.

Few believe this explanation. Why should the air temperature day after day increase with height above the ground? The scientists answer that the land around Khashabriz by chance is cooled with a subterranean lake leading to the Gulf of Oman, while the air several meters up is warmed by constant sun and mountain breezes. Caught between cold below and heat above, the air has little choice. Why should the distant castles shimmer, as if reflecting light? The scientists answer that wind is constantly stirring the air, mingling its different densities and rapidly changing its focus. There is a final question that silences the physicists. Why have they remained in Khashabriz, if the outer fortress is just illusion? They have no answer and return to their equations, just as the baker, after listening to these strange ideas, returns to his shop.

Some of the scientists have quietly abandoned their unpopular theory, without proof or disproof. Others have become philosophers, arguing that nothing exists, that all is mirage. With their converts they sit each day in the baths, the chambers of progressively warmer water, and do not notice whether their eyes are closed or open.

It is difficult for a stranger to understand the city Khashabriz. In some respects it is a normal city. Children run across the tiled courtyards chasing goats and sheep, lovers clench in darkened corners, morning shatters with the mullah's call to prayer. But in the middle of the night the empty streets are filled with sleepers' moanings, and on waking none can look directly at another, as if each person owed the other money. And the distant towers hover in the background, mixed with stone and air, daunting, mute.

Misty Patches in the Sky

Astronomy is not the oldest profession, but it is the oldest science. From 1500 B.C. in Babylon, and perhaps before, people recorded the motions of heavenly bodies for tracking the seasons, planting crops, and navigating. And as in other healthy sciences, the earliest questions ranged beyond practical applications. Outdoors, on a crystal night, celestial mysteries spill over the limits of practicality. Among the ancient riddles were the little misty patches, or nebulae, noted by the Greek astronomers Hipparchus and Ptolemy—too distant for atmospheric clouds and too diffuse for single stars. What were they?

In 1610, with his new gadget the telescope, Galileo was delighted to find that "the stars [misty patches] which have been called by every one of the astronomers up to this day, nebulous, are groups of small stars set thick together in a wonderful way, although each one of them . . . escapes our sight." Galileo had discovered star clusters, each consisting of many stars orbiting each other under their mutual gravity and created, we think, by the proximity of stars during their formations. Today, despite superior telescopes, high-speed computers, and dogged theoretical calculations, we remain baffled by the workings of star clusters.

Most beautiful and largest of star clusters are the globular clusters, which are spherical, shining balls of about a million stars all swarming about each other. Our galaxy, the Milky Way, harbors some 200. The typical globular cluster is about 100 light-years in size and about 50,000 light-years from Earth. With the naked eye you can just make out the brightest of the globular clusters, ω-Centaurus, and then only if you live in the southern hemisphere. But most globulars can be seen with even a modest telescope and offer a sensational visual spectacle rivaling the rings of Saturn.

Globular clusters have great significance to astronomy. Their stars are known to be old, so that a study of globulars may uncover secrets about the birth of the galaxy. Their distances are easily determined, so that Harlow Shapley could use globulars in 1918 to draw the first map of the Milky Way. And the structure and change of globular clusters present a rare opportunity to study the effects of gravity in a large collection of masses. Although the physical force of gravity is straightforward and well understood, its consequences within a system of many bodies can be surprisingly elaborate, just as a palette of primary colors offers little glimpse of the infinite variety of tones that may be obtained by repeated blending. The prediction of such complex behavior has been a long-standing problem in astrophysics, with applications ranging from small groups of stars to clusters of galaxies. To the student of gravitational dynamics, nature could give no better specimens than globular clusters—they are for astronomy the common amoebas of biology and the sodium chloride solutions of chemistry.

For many years our grasp of the dynamics of globulars was limited to theoretical calculations. Nevertheless, astronomers seemed to be reaching a consensus, working in quiet rooms with pencil and paper. Recently, it has been noticed that actual globular clusters up in the sky don't behave according to the homework.

Most astronomical phenomena, since the work of Kepler and Newton, have happily yielded to mathematical and physical analysis. This tradition gained strength in the first part of this century with the successful theoretical calculations by Sir Arthur Eddington and Subrahmanyan Chandrasekhar on the structure of individual stars. As far as possible, these calculations have all been confirmed by observations through the telescope, a remarkable tribute to earthbound human thought.

Following such brilliant theoretical work, it was perfectly reasonable for the Armenian astronomer Victor Ambartsumian to suggest, in 1938, a partial theory of the gravitational dynamics of globular clusters. Ambartsumian's theory held that globular clusters would slowly lose stars. As a result of the gravitational forces between stars, a small fraction of stars in a globular should continuously be accelerated up to sufficiently high velocity to escape the gravity of the cluster as a whole, heading out into empty space on a one-way trip. A globular cluster evaporates stars just as a liquid in a low-humidity room evaporates molecules. An unavoidable consequence of the outward transfer of motional energy between neighboring stars is that the central region of a globular cluster should collapse, shrinking in size and pulling the remaining stars closer and closer together. In 1958 Ivan King, now at Berkeley, did a rough quantitative calculation of such a collapse. It doesn't happen overnight. According to rough estimates, the globulars now closest to collapse will do so in another billion years, a long time by human standards but only a tenth the ages of these clusters.

Not quite trusting of the previous, rough-and-ready theory, astronomers in the late 1960s and early 1970s began simulating the gravitational dynamics of globular clusters on computers. Computer simulations of complex physical systems are now commonplace, with such terrestrial applications as weather forecasting. In effect, the computer performs an "experiment," in which a mathematical representation of a wind pattern or a globular cluster is allowed to evolve in time according to the laws of physics, sometimes galloping off into unrecognized territory. Each second of time in the computer may translate to a day or a million years in the real system being mimicked. The computer simulations of globular clusters indicated that indeed their central regions do collapse, at just about the rate predicted by the naïve theory.

How might this structure of the intellect be tested against the structure of nature? Obviously, we can't observe a globular cluster for several billion years waiting to see if and how it collapses. What we can do, however, is observe many globular clusters at different stages of development and from this infer the life story of a single globular. This is how botanists unravel the life cycle of California redwoods. Each tree lives many hundreds of years, much longer than a botanist, but by observing many trees, some just germinating, some sprouting first leaves, and others stretching grandly into old age, we can piece together the evolution of a single tree.

Recent analyses of the observed population of globular clusters produce a dismaying picture that cannot be explained by the current theory, a picture at odds with the number of globulars that should be seen at each phase of the life cycle leading to collapse. Even worse, the observations vaguely hint that some globulars have already collapsed and yet appear as if they haven't. Analysis of such a masquerade is next to impossible, as little theory exists for the evolution of a globular after collapse. A leading speculation is that some star in the collapsing center of the cluster captures a nearby star, and they orbit each other in a binary star system. Like a spinning top colliding with surrounding marbles, a rapidly rotating binary star system kicks energy to other stars and may eventually reverse the collapse of the globular in some as yet unknown way. At the very least, then, the theory is incomplete. It could be drastically oversimplified or perhaps just wrong. Scientists prefer to understand nature with as simple a theory as possible, just as Picasso said the artist should compose with as few elements as possible. In the case of the gravitational dynamics of globular clusters, unfortunately, the theory may be too simple.

A theory found too simple is particularly disappointing to astronomers. Other scientists can test embellishments of inadequate theories by quickly returning to the lab and changing the conditions of an experiment. Astronomers, however, are light-years removed from stars and galaxies and cannot do so. They must forever suffer the frustration of admiration from afar.

How Long Is a Year?

After encountering first the 6-inch Lilliputians and later the 72-foot Brobdingnagians, Gulliver wisely says, "Undoubtedly the philosophers are in the right when they tell us that nothing is great and little otherwise than by comparison."

The scientist asks what physical principles determine our familiar units of length and time. By what standards do we pronounce phenomena tall or short, fast or slow? And should we expect our natural measuring units to differ from those of living beings elsewhere in the universe, with our inch corresponding perhaps to their mile and our year to their second? Surely this should have some bearing on our ability to contact or comprehend extraterrestrials.

Let us attempt a partial answer to these questions by considering two important units of time: the rotation period of a planet, from which we derive our day; and the orbital period of a planet circling its central star, from which we derive our year. These two time periods probably figure into the sense of time for planetary beings anywhere in the universe. Sleep cycles of humans and animals follow the daily change of light and dark, and growth cycles of plants (and all higher forms in the food chain depending on plants) follow the annual change of the seasons.

At the microscopic level, natural units of time are clearly evident and determined by the fundamental properties of atoms. The hydrogen atom, for example, is a hundred-millionth of a centimeter in diameter and its electron completes ten thousand orbits around its proton every trillionth of a second. For atom-sized creatures, if such existed, this would likely provide a characteristic scale of time, a scale that would also be universal, since hydrogen atoms are believed to be the same everywhere in the universe. In contrast, the macroscopic world is a morass of details, and many familiar phenomena have no characteristic magnitude at all. Rocks, for example. They come in all sizes, ranging from a ten-millionth of a centimeter (the size of several molecules of silicon-dioxide) up to 10 million centimeters (the largest object that can hold a nonspherical shape against its own gravity). Ocean waves arrive ashore at intervals ranging from much shorter than a second to several hours. Despite the enormous possible range of many macroscopic phenomena, some plausible assumptions and scientific arguments suggest that the lengths of the day and the year on all habitable planets are remarkably similar.

Begin with the day, the period of time for a planet to complete a rotation. Although we still lack a good theory of the formation of solar systems, it is generally agreed that planets condense out of a rotating system of gas and particles. There is a maximum rotation rate of any large body, at which point the outward rotational acceleration overwhelms the inward gravitational acceleration and causes the body to break apart. Since it is observed that most nascent astrophysical systems have a great deal of rotation, we would expect planets to form with a rotation not much below the maximum possible. Once formed, a planet holds its rate of spin unless acted on by outside forces. The maximum rate corresponds to a rotation period that depends only on the mean planetary density; that is, all planets with the same mean density—even with vastly different masses—should theoretically have about the same rotation periods. In our own solar system, which is the only available laboratory for checking this idea, all the planets have nearly equal density of a few grams per cubic centimeter. This translates to a predicted rotation period of several hours. In fact, six of the nine planets have observed rotation periods between ten and twenty-five hours, while their masses range over a factor of several thousand. The three exceptions to this delightful agreement with the theory have almost certainly been affected by external forces. Mercury, with a rotation period of 59 days, has been influenced by the sun's tidal forces; Venus, at 244 days, has been tidally locked by Earth; and Pluto, at six days, has probably been affected by a recently discovered large and nearby moon.

It's not surprising that the planets in our solar system have approximately the same density. All ordinary solids and liquids, from sand to water, have about the same density, determined by the weight and closeness of their constituent atoms. To within a factor of two or three, an atom of silicon has the same weight and size as an atom of oxygen, set by the masses of the proton and electron, charge of the electron, and Planck's quantum constant. These are "fundamental constants" of nature, which, we believe, have identical values everywhere in the universe. As a consequence, the length of the day should be nearly the same everywhere in the universe.

What determines the length of our year? It is the time it takes Earth to orbit its central star, the sun. How long or short might be the year on other planets, orbiting other stars? Since the work of Kepler and Newton, we've known that the orbital period of a planet depends on the mass and distance of the central star gravitationally attracting it. Offhand, we might expect these two quantities could have arbitrary values, leading to an enormous possible variation in planetary years. However, this is not the case.

The key idea is habitability. Consider a planet located at some distance from a central star shining with some luminosity (rate of energy output). Let us assume the planet receives its heat from the star. Then, the higher the luminosity of the star, the hotter will be the planet, and the greater the separation between planet and star, the colder the planet. For the planet to be habitable, however, the temperature had better not be much greater than that which catalyzes the reactions of organic molecules, or else the molecular innards of any life forms will be disrupted. But the temperature should also not be much lower than this value, because biochemical processes proceed at an exponentially slower rate with decreasing temperature, a well known result in chemistry. Under these assumptions, the development of life restricts planetary temperatures to near 100° centigrade (a bit warm for human comfort, but in the right ball park). This is about the temperature at which all large organic molecules on Earth, and everywhere in the universe, disrupt. Again, the magnitude is set by the fundamental properties of atoms and molecules.

Demanding a "favorable" temperature on habitable planets forces a particular star-to-planet distance for each possible stellar luminosity. Now it happens that the luminosity of most stars is almost completely fixed by their masses. More massive stars are more luminous. Everything, therefore, hinges on the mass of the central star. Specify that, and the stellar luminosity is unavoidably determined, the distance to the hypothetical habitable planet is determined, and the length of the year is determined. For good physical reasons, the masses of stars are limited to a relatively narrow range about that of our own sun. Stars of more than about thirty times the mass of our sun are unable to hold together under the pressure of their own radiation, and would-be stars of less than about a tenth the mass of our sun never achieve high enough interior temperatures to ignite their nuclear fuel. Indeed, few stars have ever been observed outside these limits.

Unfortunately, a range of possible stellar masses from a tenth to ten times our sun's mass translates into a rather large range of stellar luminosities, from a thousandth to a thousand times our sun's. However, the requirement of conditions favorable to life imposes some further restrictions. High luminosity stars are relatively scarce, and, furthermore, exhaust their nuclear fuel in a relatively short period of time. The evolution of life on a star-heated planet may well require a certain minimum of time. If we require the nuclear life of the central star to be at least a billion years, the approximate time for life to arise on Earth, then the stellar luminosity must be less than about a hundred times that of our sun. On the other hand, if a star's luminosity is lower than about one hundredth that of our sun, most of its energy will be emitted at infrared wavelengths of light and unable to activate the chemical reactions involved in photosynthesis. Many biologists believe the replenishment of organic molecules by photosynthesis is a must for the survival of life forms.

Combining these arguments and assumptions, at last, limits the probable variation for the year on habitable planets to between about a tenth and ten times our Earthly year. In the grand scheme of things, this is a remarkably slender interval. Happily for us, the calculations allow our own existence.

It is tempting to speculate on the implications of a universal year for biology. Foremost is the change of the seasons. Winter is colder than summer because the wintery latitudes are tilted away from the sun during that portion of Earth's orbit. At least six of the nine planets in our solar system have rotation axes tilted from their orbital planes as much as Earth's, so that we may expect annual planetary seasons to be a general phenomenon. Especially sensitive to light and temperature variations are plants, which grow and reproduce on a cycle tuned to the year. The year thus becomes a significant time scale for all higher forms of the food chain, ultimately dependent on plants and photosynthesis. We might further conjecture that it is not a coincidence that the life span of mice and men lies between one and a hundred years. Indeed, almost all higher animals on Earth have life spans of roughly a year, or ten years. Why should the year be a relevant time scale here? Why not ten seconds? Why not ten thousand years? When plants first emerged from the constant sea, some billion years ago, they had to adapt to a seasonally changing environment. Advancing life forms may have continued to lengthen the duration of their life cycle, as complexity increased, until the seasonal barrier was reached. In this manner, perhaps, the year was built into biological machinery as a natural life span, or at least a reproductive time scale. Such a conjecture offers little understanding of the aging process, a long outstanding and difficult mystery in biology, but does emphasize the possible deep significance of a universal year.

Much of this must be considered as unproven speculation. No beings from other worlds have come to testify, and it is certainly possible to imagine circumstances in which our assumptions would be violated—for example, by life forms composed of sound waves instead of large molecules, or heated by planetary radioactivity instead of by a central star. We must wait and continue to search. What is most interesting, I think, are the questions themselves, the measuring units we take for granted, and the scientific arguments we make, on our one small planet, that have some bearing on these questions. And if we do discover some extraterrestrial Brobdingnagians, the chances seem fair their scale of time will be similar to ours.

Ironland

[One evening not long ago, as I sat quietly reading by the fireside, a hooded stranger knocked on my door, handed me a crumpled missive, and quickly left. I would not have placed much credibility in his curious story, which I reprint below, had I not later noticed the wood was crushed where he brushed the door frame.]

I have been walking the streets for days, virtually blind, in search of another creature of my kind. How I came here through the vastness of space I cannot tell, but I feel compelled to share something of my home. I will call our world Ironland, not because we call it so, but to make its nature clearer to you. In Ironland everything is made of iron. No other elements exist. Picture a land with no air, no rain, no grass; no oxygen or hydrogen or carbon. Imagine a planet with only iron and what can be fashioned from iron. Knowing no other way of life, we consider this state of affairs perfectly natural.

Our world is far simpler than yours. First of all, chemistry is unheard of, there being no other elements available to react with iron. I have been astonished at the myriad chemical phenomena you have: photosynthesis, battery power, taste. Not even our science-fiction writers have imagined such things. Still, we enjoy some compensations. You will grasp at once how durable our structures are, compared to yours. Without corrosion and decay, our splendid houses stand forever and maintain their initial gray-white color. I would think that architects in your world, especially those anxious that their buildings last a thousand years, must find oxidation a frightful nuisance. Indeed, aging of all kinds proceeds more swiftly on a world with chemistry, although this still does not explain why your creatures rarely live beyond 100 Earthly years.

You may wonder what distinguishes the animate from the inanimate in Ironland, and I will tell you. We experience nature on its simplest terms and have decided that life, in its essence, consists of information—and mechanisms for expressing that information. Now iron, as you know, has magnetic properties. Some years ago, our scientists discovered that the microscopic magnetic regions inside our living matter are oriented according to definite patterns. That is, if you think of each of these regions as being a magnet, then the little north poles in animate matter point up or down in very particular arrangements, analogous to the sequences of dots and dashes in your Morse code or the on and off switches in your computers. Any piece of information can be reduced to such a sequence and stored. In lifeless forms, like rocks and hammers, the tiny internal magnets point haphazardly, with little relationship to each other. No greater magnetic information resides within a rock than in a word of letters taken randomly from the alphabet.

Magnetism in our society is akin to money in yours. We base our status on it. But the Board of Magnetometers, curse them, has more or less dictated the system. The lower classes, like welders, are permitted an overall magnetic field of no more than 100 gauss. (So that you will understand me, I have converted our magnetic units to yours. One gauss, if I am not mistaken, is about twice the magnetic field strength of your planet.) The middle classes, like sculptors and doctors, are allowed up to 1,000 gauss. Some members of the upper classes—I know one politician in particular—boast magnetic fields as high as 10,000 gauss and more. Now, I'll take you into my confidence, but this must never get back to my world. Some of us have noticed that with increasing status comes increasing stupidity. Eventually we realized why. You see, to get high overall magnetization, the microscopic magnetic regions within a person must line up, with most of the little north poles pointing in the same direction. Otherwise, they'll partly cancel each other, reducing the overall magnetic strength. But as a greater number of the microscopic magnets are restricted in their orientation, less are available to store information. It's like restricting a larger and larger fraction of the letters in a word to be the single letter *a*. The extreme case is when all the microscopic magnets point in the same direction, producing a maximum magnetic field of about 20,000 gauss. At this point, all intelligence has been abandoned in favor of status.

I myself carry around 300 gauss, which in my opinion is enough to make ends meet but not so much as to

go to my head. I am a writer. Often, I have felt grateful for this one modest talent, as I am somewhat homely and definitely lacking in social graces. My dear mate was recently certified at 310 gauss, although she deserves more. I noticed her fine mettle the first day we met, at the foundry. When I say noticed, you must appreciate that all our sense perceptions are magnetic and operate on much the same principles as some of your metal detectors.

I suppose I'd better explain something about our sexuality. Roughly speaking, your maleness and femaleness correspond in our land to the north and south poles of a magnet. But since any magnet has both poles, every person in Ironland is bisexual. Depending on how you're standing or sitting in relation to someone else, you can find that individual extremely attractive or repulsive. As you can imagine, courtships have to be handled with great delicacy, and you can still slip into an awkward position after many years of marriage.

There is a saying, on our world, that wayward spouses can usually be turned around. But sometimes one encounters a whole group of disagreeable, misdirected people, and that leads to war. Regrettably, warfare in Ironland suffers for want of strong weapons. Without chemical reactions, we lack chemical explosives. Oh, what I could do with some of your gunpowder or TNT back home.

Much worse, we've failed miserably to build nuclear explosives. I must admit, however, the reason is not without its fascination. As you well know, the particles in atomic nuclei interact with two kinds of forces: a repulsive electrical force, acting between the protons, and an attractive nuclear force, acting between both protons and neutrons. The first force is like a compressed spring while the second like a stretched spring, each poised to snap back to its natural position, releasing energy in the process. Unfortunately, the two kinds of springs pull in opposite directions, so when energy is gained from one it is lost from the other. To get an explosion, of course, more energy must be released than absorbed. Your fission bombs produce energy by splitting nuclei. This method only works for the heavy nuclei, like uranium. On the other hand, for light nuclei, such as hydrogen, net energy is produced by joining them together. You call weapons made in this way fusion bombs. Now that I understand these things, it is not so remarkable there should be a special atomic nucleus unluckily caught right in the middle—neither light enough to yield net energy by fusion, nor heavy enough to do so by fission. In effect, its stretched and compressed springs completely cancel themselves in either direction. That barren and singular nucleus is none other than iron, the sole element of our world.

Nevertheless, being people of some intelligence and resourcefulness, we've found ways of doing away with each other. One can always heat an enemy to oblivion. When the temperature of iron exceeds 768 Celsius, still well below its melting point, the substance loses all its magnetism. Under such heat, the tiny internal magnets become totally disoriented. It is death by loss of all knowledge, sense of self, and status—but without destruction of material. Rather humane, don't you agree?

We are a cultured people. Our poets cannot write of oceans, but they have mused on the latent stillness of low temperatures, the texture of a cubic lattice shifted, the inner seething of magnetic storms. Our artists cannot paint, but they have created winding sculptures whose forces tingle helically. Confined to the most primitive form of the material universe, we have yet risen to great heights of expression.

Now you know a bit about Ironland. I would write far more, but time does not permit. Already, I am rusting in your wretched air and must depart. Good-bye.

Jam Tomorrow

It is now more than three hundred years since Blaise Pascal and Pierre de Fermat pioneered the mathematical theory of probability—after millennia of thoughtless gambling, going back, perhaps, to the days when our ancestors first came off all fours.

Applications of the theory to human affairs is another matter. Weighing the odds in personal decisions involves a morass of perceptive and emotional factors seeping past the neat analysis of binomial theorems, combinatorics, and Gaussian distributions. What were the perceptions of the citizens of Tacoma, Washington, who were recently asked to choose between an uncertain risk of cancer from arsenic in the air and the loss of 800 jobs from the closing of a copper smelting factory?

Such haunting decisions may not be easier when the uncertainties are more certain. Four of the five .30-30 deer rifles used in the 1977 execution of murderer Gary Gilmore were carefully loaded with steel-jacketed shells. The fifth held a blank. No one knew which rifles held live shells, which one held the blank. Did each of those riflemen measure his personal responsibility for Gilmore's death as eighty percent? Would it have made a difference with one blank in ten, or one in three?

Pascal and Fermat, both mathematicians, were concerned not with problems of life and death, but with games of chance. Here, all is clean and analytical. To illustrate, if two dice are tossed onto the table, what is the probability of getting a sum of eight points? Central to answering this question, and in fact all questions of probability, are the notions of randomness and independent events.

First, randomness. If a die is thrown haphazardly, the event is considered random and its outcome depends only on the intrinsic properties of the die itself. In the case of an unloaded die, each of its six sides is identical in shape and weight and thus has equal chance of landing face up: one in six or $\frac{1}{6}$. (The probabilities of all possible outcomes must of course add up to 1.)

Now we come to independent events. When two dice are thrown, the two events are considered independent if each is separately random. The outcome of the second throw is not influenced by that of the first. Many people, including some of my relatives, believe the probability of getting a heads after nine flips of tails is much larger than $\frac{1}{2}$, an example of the erroneous "law of averages," which, if true, would imply some mysterious physical force acting on the coin in that tenth flip.

We can now answer the original puzzle, assuming the two throws are random. For each of the six possible faces coming up on the first die, there are six possible faces on the second, making a total of thirty-six equally probable combinations. Five of these combinations give a sum of eight points. (This will be left as an exercise for the reader.) Thus the probability is five in thirty-six, or $\frac{5}{36}$. Clear and antiseptic.

Applying the odds to the human condition began in England. In 1662, John Graunt published the first book on vital statistics, *Natural and Political Observations ... Made upon the Bills of Mortality,* recording the numbers of births, deaths, and various diseases in London from 1604 to 1661. In 1632, for example, we learn that 1,797 people died of consumption, 8 of plague, 5 from lunatique, and 38 of the king's evil, as well as the figures for 59 other causes of death. Graunt concludes by giving the fraction of people who died from particular casualties. It's but a short step from fractions to probabilities.

In 1693 the first life insurance tables were published by Edmond Halley, the same fellow who, in his more serious diversions, charted Halley's comet and persuaded Newton to proceed with the *Principia.* Halley acknowledges his debt to Captain John Graunt right from the start. He then goes on to show how a record of the number of living people at each age can be used to determine the probability of various longevities and the proper way to charge life insurance premiums. One of his examples: the probability of a 40-year-old man *not* living at least another seven years is the decrease in the number of people between ages 40 and 47 divided by the number of people at age 40. For the town of Breslaw (Poland), upon which Halley based his statistics, there were 377 people of age 47 and 445 of age 40, giving a 15 percent chance of not surviving that age interval. What Halley realized was that, even in ignorance of the many complex biological factors determining aging and death, a long enough historical record permits one to make sensible statistical projections into the future. This differs from dice-throwing problems, where one can compute the various probabilities a priori, without a log of the last ten thousand throws, because one knows all about the properties of a die. Both methods have their validity.

We cannot overestimate the social significance of Graunt's and Halley's works. Although dealing with statistical data, as opposed to the elegant abstractions of Pascal and Fermat, they dared quantify the life cycles of human beings. Advising a friend how to gamble seems trifling beside informing her she has two chances in three to live through the year.

Most people, I suspect, have a deep-seated reluctance to welcome probabilities into their private lives. At least since the Greeks, mankind has harbored a passion for knowing some things with certainty. Probabilities, by definition, shimmer in a mist of uncertainty. Einstein contributed little to science in the last three decades of his life, in large part because he could never accept the probabalistic nature of the emerging quantum physics. "God does not play dice," he insisted. Thomas Aquinas, who spent a lifetime observing the limits of human knowledge and still wondered if he knew anything with certainty, is said to have laid down his pen for the last time with the words "All that I have written is as straw."

Probabilities, by definition, are impersonal. Who is the 0.2 in the 2.2 children per family? Who should not drive on Labor Day weekend, when ten in each million cars on the road will have fatal crashes?

Still, we must cope with these numbers. And in a modern world of diffuse liabilities and social dependences, a world of PCBs and toxic wastes and acid rain, statistical considerations thrust themselves upon us. A recent court case in California hints that the legal profession, our guardian of truth in human affairs, may finally be inching its considerable inertia in this direction. In 1980 Judith Sindell, a victim of the cancer-causing synthetic estrogen diethylstilbestrol (DES), successfully sued Abbott Laboratories, the Upjohn Company, and three other companies for producing the drug. All parties acknowledged the impossibility of ever identifying which drug company had manufactured the particular batch of DES used by Sindell's mother, but it was most likely at least one of the five. If ever there was a situation where some concept of statistical liability should apply, this was it. Before Sindell, however, it was standard legal practice to throw out any case where the plaintiff could not prove her case against a *specific* defendant. Before Sindell, each of the five defendants could have claimed, "Hey, it wasn't me, it was some other company" and gotten off the hook. The logic of this traditional defense reminds me of the White Queen promising Alice twopence a week and jam every other day, explaining "The rule is, jam tomorrow and jam yesterday—but never jam today."

We can only hope, with our fingers crossed, that the Sindell case will hold its high ground. That would be a needed beginning. Eventually, the law might also confront the more difficult question of apportioning liability when the cause as well as the defendant is essentially statistical. Here might fit the melange of environmental hazards, many of which can cause the same injuries but with untraceable origins.

I've always marveled at the way medical doctors take these issues in stride, soberly telling their patients the chances, deciding whether to operate, weighing the possible outcomes. Day by day, doctors must convert the odds into yes or no decisions for single human beings. Somehow, at least on a professional level, they have learned to ponder probabilities and real people within the same compartment of their minds.

Notes and References

TIME TRAVEL AND PAPA JOE'S PIPE

There are numerous semipopular books on the Special
Theory of Relativity. An amusing one at the very
introductory level is George Gamow, *Mister Tompkins
in Paperback* (New York: Cambridge University
Press, 1967). One requiring a little mathematical
knowledge is E. F. Taylor and J. A. Wheeler, *Space-
time Physics* (San Francisco: W. H. Freeman and Co.,
1963). In this latter book, Minkowski diagrams are
used abundantly, under the name "spacetime
diagrams."

For popular introductions to the General Theory of Relativity, see Robert Geroch, *General Relativity from A
to B* (Chicago: University of Chicago Press, 1978); or
the article by Larry Smarr and William Press in
American Scientist (vol. 66, 1978), p. 72.

$I = V/R$

The calculations by the two Japanese scientists on gravitational dynamics: M. Saito and M. Yoshizawa, *Astrophysics and Space Science* (vol. 41, 1976), p. 63.

The statement attributed to Einstein is referred to by I. Bernard Cohen in "Franklin and Newton," *Memoirs of the American Philosophical Society* (vol. 43, 1956), p. 43.

Biographical information on Ohm, Volta, Fourier, Maxwell, and Drude may be found in *Dictionary of Scientific Biography* (New York: Scribners, 1974). Additional information on Ohm is in the paper by E. Lommel in *Annual Report of the Board of Regents of the Smithsonian Institution* (July 1891), p. 247 (Washington, D.C.: Government Printing Office, 1893).

The quote by Delbrück is in *Science News* (vol. 119, 1981), p. 268.

THE LOSS OF THE PROTON

A recent review of proton decay may be found in S. Weinberg, *Scientific American* (vol. 244, 1981), p. 64. The current status of the Irvine-Michigan-Brookhaven proton decay experiment in the United States is discussed in L. R. Sulak, "Waiting for the Proton to Decay," *American Scientist* (vol. 70, 1982), p. 616.

The monitored material in the Kolar Gold Fields has about 10^{32} protons. Assuming a proton lifetime of 10^{31} years, this yields about 1 decay per month.

Taking a volume of 10^{-3} cm^3 per grain of sand, a depth
of 10^3 cm for a typical beach, and an equivalent
beach area of the entire Earth's surface, I get $\sim 10^{25}$
grains of sand on Earth.

A recent summary of grand unified theories is H. Georgi,
Scientific American (vol. 244, 1981), p. 48.

H. Georgi, H. R. Quinn, and S. Weinberg, *Physical Review
Letters* (vol. 33, 1974), p. 451.

The partially unified theory that links the electromagnetic
and weak nuclear force, called SU(2) $\times$ U(1), was
developed by Glashow, Weinberg, and Salam. Some
of their earliest papers are S. Glashow, *Nuclear Physics*
(vol. 22, 1961), p. 579; S. Weinberg, *Physical Review
Letters* (vol. 19, 1967), p. 1264; A. Salam, in *Elementary
Particle Physics,* N. Svartholm, ed. (Stockholm:
Almquist and Wiksels, 1968).

Some of the important experiments helping to confirm the
Glashow-Salam-Weinberg model are reported in F.
Reines, H. S. Gurr, and H. W. Sobel, *Physical Review
Letters* (vol. 37, 1976), p. 315; W. Lee et al., *Physical
Review Letters* (vol. 37, 1976), p. 186. More definitive
experimental confirmation of this theory was the re-
cent discovery of the W particle, a charged coun-
terpart of the Z_0, reported by Carlo Rubbia at the
January 1983 meeting of the American Physical So-
ciety in New York.

An early version of Einstein's unified theory, linking the
electromagnetic and gravitational force, is in A. Einstein and W. Mayer, *Sitzungsberichte* (Berlin: Akade-
mie Berlin, 1931), p. 257. A final version is in A.
Einstein, *The Meaning of Relativity,* third ed., (Princeton, N.J.: Princeton University Press, 1950).

The statement from Rilke occurs in Rainer Maria Rilke, Letter 4, *Letters to a Young Poet* (New York: Norton, 1954).

OTHER ROOMS

P. C. Peters and J. Mathews, "Gravitational Radiation from Point Masses in a Keplerian Orbit," *Physical Review* (vol. 131, 1963), p. 435.

J. Mathews and R. L. Walker, *Mathematical Methods of Physics* (New York: W. A. Benjamin, Inc., 1970).

F. Dyson, *Disturbing the Universe* (New York: Harper and Row, 1979), p. 9.

ORIGINS

Two popular books on cosmology are J. Silk, *The Big Bang: Creation and Evolution of the Universe* (San Francisco: W. H. Freeman and Co., 1980); and S. Weinberg, *The First Three Minutes* (New York: Basic Books, 1976).

The binding energies of carbon and nitrogen are 92 million and 128 million electron volts, respectively.

A. S. Eddington, *Report of the Eighty-Eighth Meeting of the British Association for the Advancement of Science* (1920), p. 34.

For a nice discussion of the creation of elements in stars, see "The Origin of the Elements," by William A. Fowler, *Scientific American* (vol. 195, September 1956), p. 82. A more technical discussion is D. D. Clayton,

Principles of Stellar Evolution and Nucleosynthesis (New York: McGraw-Hill, 1968).

A review of stellar models and a comparison between theory and observations is I. Iben, Jr., *Annual Reviews of Astronomy and Astrophysics* (vol. 5, 1967), p. 571.

A recent review of the observations of supernovae spectra, is J. B. Oke and L. Searle, *Annual Review of Astronomy and Astrophysics* (vol. 12, 1974), p. 315. Recent calculations of nucleosynthesis in supernovae and comparisons to observations are in M. D. Johnston and P. C. Joss, *The Astrophysical Journal* (vol. 242, 1980), p. 1124.

Gaseous matter in the expanding universe first became unstable to gravitational condensation, leading to the ultimate formation of stars and galaxies, when the pressure of the ambient radiation became negligible. This occurred when the universe was between a hundred thousand and a million years old.

NOTHING BUT THE TRUTH

Italo Calvino, *The Path to the Nest of Spiders* (New York: Ecco Press, 1976).

Summaries of Landau's life and work may be found in the *Dictionary of Scientific Biography* (New York: Scribners, 1974); and in the lengthy preface, by E. M. Lifshitz, to L. D. Landau and E. M. Lifshitz, *Course in Theoretical Physics, Volume 1, Mechanics* (Oxford, England: Pergamon Press, 1976). Landau's nameplate is mentioned in this latter article.

The wonderful phrase "Nonsense always remains nonsense" was known as Landau's Conservation Theorem and was related to me by the mathematical astronomer S. Chandrasekhar.

The paper "On the Theory of Stars" was published in *Physikalische Zeitschrift der Sowjetunion* (vol. 1, 1932), p. 285, and is reprinted in H. Gursky and R. Ruffini, eds., *Neutron Stars, Black Holes, and Binary X-Ray Sources* (Dordrecht, Netherlands: Reidel, 1975), p. 271.

The key elements of quantum mechanics necessary for Landau's calculations were the Pauli Exclusion Principle (1925) and the Heisenberg Uncertainty Principle (1927).

A popular version of Chandrasekhar's calculations and Eddington's reception to them is given in J. Tierney's article in *Science 82* (vol. 3, 1982), p. 68. Eddington's remarks were published in A. S. Eddington, *The Observatory* (vol. 58, 1935), p. 38. A history of the concept of black holes, at a somewhat technical level, is in S. Chandrasekhar, *Contemporary Physics* (vol. 14, 1974), p. 1.

A discussion of Einstein's theory of gravity, including its 1917 modification, may be found in S. Weinberg, *Gravitation and Cosmology* (New York: Wiley, 1972).

J. Weber, "Evidence for Discovery of Gravitational Radiation," *Physical Review Letters* (vol. 22, 1969), p. 1320.

P. B. Price et al., "Evidence for Detection of a Moving Magnetic Monopole," *Physical Review Letters* (vol. 35, 1975), p. 487. A critical review of this work, including the theory of monopoles and alternative interpretations of Price's data, can be found in *Physics Today,* October 1975. The theory of magnetic monopoles was first developed by P. A. M. Dirac, *Proceedings of the Royal Society* (London, Ser. A, vol. 133, 1931), p. 60.

Francis Bacon, *The New Organum,* F. H. Anderson, ed. (Indianapolis: Bobbs-Merrill, 1960), Book 1, 49.

For a discussion of the catastrophic or "punctuated equilibrium" theory of evolutionary change, see chapter 17 of S. J. Gould, *The Panda's Thumb* (New York: Norton, 1980).

Feynman's commencement address was at California Institute of Technology in June 1974.

Science on the Right Side of the Brain

An introductory article on hemispheric specialization is R. J. Trotter, "The Other Hemisphere," *Science News* (vol. 109, 1976), p. 218. Then see R. J. Sperry in *The Psychophysiology of Thinking,* F. J. McGuigan and R. A. Schoonover, eds. (New York: Academic Press, 1973).

An article on Broca may be found in the *Dictionary of Scientific Biography* (New York: Scribners, 1974).

Rudyard Kipling, *Verses* (London: Hodder and Stoughton, 1927).

Betty Edwards, *Drawing on the Right Side of the Brain* (Los Angeles: J. P. Tarcher, Inc., 1979).

Mendeleyev and Newlands are discussed in D. Q. Posin, *Mendeleyev* (New York: McGraw-Hill, 1948), especially page 169, and in J. A. R. Newlands, "On the

Law of Octaves," *Chemical News* (vol. 12, 1865), p. 83.

The Stanford physicist was Leonard Schiff, and the Schiff Conjecture, first published in the *American Journal of Physics* (vol. 28, 1960), p. 340, is that all theories of gravity satisfying the weak equivalence principle must be metric theories. My proof of the conjecture, under restricted conditions, is in A. P. Lightman and D. L. Lee, *Physical Review D* (vol. 8, 1973), p. 363.

On the Dizzy Edge

A nice description of the Baconian and Galilean approaches to science can be found in P. B. Medawar, *Advice to a Young Scientist* (New York: Harper and Row, 1979).

Bertrand Russell, *An Inquiry into Meaning and Truth* (Baltimore: Penguin Books, 1962).

Much of the work on the anthropic principle, including the values of the nuclear and cosmological parameters, is quantitatively summarized in the review article by B. J. Carr and M. J. Rees, *Nature* (vol. 278, 1979), p. 605, and qualitatively summarized in less breadth by G. Gale, *Scientific American* (vol. 245, 1981), p. 154.

The nuclear parameter discussed is technically the "strong coupling constant." For a large value of this parameter, the existence of bound states of ^{2}He would have converted all hydrogen to helium in the cosmological fusion reactions of the early universe.

The cosmological parameter discussed is technically the Hubble constant divided by the square root of the mean mass density. Another cosmological parameter, the "cosmological constant," and its relationship to the anthropic principle, has been discussed recently by S. W. Hawking in *Quantum Gravity,* C. J. Isham and M. J. Duff, eds. (Cambridge, England: Cambridge University Press, 1982). A new theory of cosmology, the Inflationary Universe, has proposed a possible explanation for the value of the cosmological parameter, independent of initial conditions. See M. M. Waldrop's article in *Science 84* (vol. 5, no. 1, 1984), p. 44; and A. H. Guth, *Physical Review D* (vol. 23, 1981), p. 347.

For a discussion of synthesis of elements in stars, see my essay "Origins," in this book and references therein.

R. H. Dicke, *Nature* (vol. 192, 1961), p. 440.

B. Carter, in *Confrontation of Cosmological Theories with Observational Data,* M. S. Longair, ed. (Dordrecht, Netherlands: Reidel, 1974).

For a theoretical discussion of living structures under very different conditions than our present universe see F. J. Dyson, *Reviews of Modern Physics* (vol. 51, 1979), p. 447.

Rubáiyát of Omar Khayyám, translated into English by E. Fitzgerald (New York: Random House, 1947).

J. A. Wheeler in Chapter 44 of *Gravitation* by C. W. Misner, K. S. Thorne, and J. A. Wheeler (San Francisco: W. H. Freeman and Co., 1973). See also J. A. Wheeler in *Foundational Problems in the Special Sciences,* Butts and Hintikka, eds. (Dordrecht, Netherlands: Reidel, 1977).

E. O. Wilson, *Sociobiology* (Cambridge, Mass.: Harvard University Press, Belknap Press, 1980).

For a popular discussion of hemispheric specialization in the brain, see R. J. Trotter in *Science News* (vol. 109, 1976), p. 218. For a more technical discussion, see R. W. Sperry in *The Psychophysiology of Thinking,* F. J. McGuigan and R. A. Schoonover, eds. (New York: Academic Press, 1973).

See the discussion, in layperson's terms, in E. Nagel and J. R. Newman, *Gödel's Proof* (New York: New York University Press, 1958).

THE SPACE TELESCOPE

For additional information on the Space Telescope, see J. N. Bahcall and L. Spitzer, Jr., *Scientific American* (vol. 247, July 1982), p. 40.

Jules Verne, *Cinq semaines en balloon* (New York: French and European Publications, Inc., 1976).

Jules Verne, *From the Earth to the Moon,* reproduction of the 1874 edition (Mattituck, New York: Amereon Ltd, n.d.)

H. Oberth, *Die Rakete du den Planetraumen* (Munich: R. Oldenbourg-Verlag, 1923).

Details of the Einstein Observatory, originally named HEAO-B, may be found in R. Giacconi et al., *The Astrophysical Journal* (vol. 230, 1979), p. 540.

A popular introduction to cosmology is J. Silk, *The Big Bang* (San Francisco: W. H. Freeman and Co., 1980); a good discussion of the cosmic distance ladder is S.

Weinberg, *Gravitation and Cosmology* (New York: Wiley, 1972), ch. 14.

For an introduction to black holes, see W. Sullivan, *Black Holes* (New York: Warner Books, 1980). The special distribution of stars around a massive black hole was first discussed by P. J. E. Peebles in *General Relativity and Gravitation* (vol. 3, 1972), p. 63.

Contributions of Boeing Aerospace to the Space Telescope were discussed in the February 4, 1982, issue of *Boeing News.*

Estimates of the staffing of the Space Telescope Science Institute were reported in *Institutional Arrangements for the Space Telescope, Report of a Study at Woods Hole* (National Academy of Sciences, 1976).

Francis Bacon's vision of a technological world occurs in *The New Atlantis.* One edition of this is Volume 3 of *The Harvard Classics,* C. W. Eliot, ed. (New York: P. F. Collier and Son, 1909).

For a recent discussion of particle accelerators, see R. R. Wilson, *Physics Today* (vol. 34, 1981), p. 86.

Lewis Mumford, *The Myth of the Machine* (New York: Harcourt, Brace, Jovanovich, 1967).

M. Harwit, *Cosmic Discovery* (New York: Basic Books, 1981).

IS THE EARTH ROUND OR FLAT?

Aristotle's arguments that the Earth is round were published in *De Caelo* ("on the heavens"), translated by W.K.C. Guthrie (Cambridge, Mass.: Harvard University Press, Loeb Classical Library, 1939), and found in pages 89–99 of *Theories of the Universe,* M. K. Munitz, ed. (New York: Free Press, 1957).

A discussion of Eratosthenes' calculations, with a guide to early Greek references (none of his original works remain), can be found in J.L.E. Dreyer, *A History of Astronomy from Thales to Kepler* (New York: Dover, 1953).

An English translation of Sacrobosco's book is by Lynn Thorndike, *The Sphere of Sacrobosco and its Commentators* (Chicago: University of Chicago Press, 1949). A recent discussion of Sacrobosco's *Sphaera,* including some of the diagrams from the book, can be found in Owen Gingerich's article in *Sky and Telescope* (January 1981), p. 4.

RELATIVITY FOR THE TABLE

A nice little book at the qualitative level is *The ABC of Relativity,* by Bertrand Russell (New York: New American Library, 1969). More quantitative, but still full of physical examples, is *Spacetime Physics,* by Edwin F. Taylor and John A. Wheeler (San Francisco: W. H. Freeman and Co., 1966).

STUDENTS AND TEACHERS

Wheeler's recollections of his student days with Bohr are taken from *Nuclear Physics in Retrospect,* R. H.

Stuewer, ed. (Minneapolis: University of Minnesota Press, 1979). Additional biographical information about Wheeler, including comments by his colleagues and students, may be found in the introduction to *Magic Without Magic: John Archibald Wheeler,* J. R. Klauder, ed. (San Francisco: W. H. Freeman and Co., 1972).

Lineages and numerous statistics of Nobel Prize winners can be found in H. Zuckerman, *Scientific Elite* (New York: Macmillan, 1977).

A good introduction to Paxton's work and the Boston school, including biographical sketches of Paxton and Gammell, is William McGregor Paxton, ed. *E. W. Lee, R. H. Gammell, and M. F. Krause* (Indianapolis: Indianapolis Museum of Art, 1979).

H. A. Krebs, "The Making of a Scientist," *Nature* (vol. 215, 1967), p. 1441.

Gammell's quote regarding Paxton comes from an unpublished manuscript.

The photo of Paxton's class is in William McGregor Paxton, op. cit., p. 114.

Wheeler's remarks at the Einstein statue dedication are in *Letter to Members, National Academy of Sciences* (vol. 9, no. 3, June 1979), p. 1.

IF BIRDS CAN FLY, WHY OH WHY CAN'T I?

This essay was partly inspired by J.B.S. Haldane's beautiful essay "On Being the Right Size," which discusses, at the qualitative level, various limitations on biological sizes imposed by nature. Haldane's essay was first published in his book *Possible Worlds* (New York: Harper and Row, 1928) and is reprinted in *The World of Mathematics*, vol. 2, James R. Newman, ed. (New York: Simon and Schuster, 1956).

In all numerical calculations, I assumed a density of solid matter of one gram per cubic centimeter, a density of air of 0.001 grams per cubic centimeter, a typical lift coefficient of one, and a typical drag-to-lift ratio of 0.05.

To obtain the power required for Icarus to fly, I assumed a total wing area of 12,000 square centimeters and a total weight of 150 pounds.

The expression relating fluid speed, density, and pressure is called Bernoulli's Equation and can be found in introductory physics books.

"Bird Aerodynamics" by John N. Storer, in *Scientific American* (vol. 186, April 1952), p. 24.

The statements regarding Leonardo da Vinci may be found in *The Life, Times, and Art of Leonardo*, Enzo Orlandi, ed. (New York: Crescent Books, 1965).

"The Work Output of Animals" by D. R. Wilkie, in *Nature* (vol. 183, 1959), p. 1515.

"Man-powered Flight as a Sport," by K. Sherman, in *Nature* (vol. 238, 1972), p. 195.

Details of the Gossamer Condor may be found in "A Dream of Wings—via Feet," in *Science News* (September 3, 1977), p. 149.

The mean body area of an object of so many pounds is defined as the area of a solid sphere of the same weight and density.

COSMIC NATURAL SELECTION?

H. L. Mckinney, ed., *Lamarck to Darwin: Contributions to Evolutionary Biology 1809-1859* (Lawrence, Kan.: Coronado Press, 1971), pp. 69-82, 89-98.

G. L. Stebbins, *The Basis of Progressive Evolution* (Chapel Hill: University of North Carolina Press, 1969), ch. 5.

Isaac Asimov, *Foundation Triology* (New York: Avon, 1974).

G. K. O'Neill, *High Frontier* (Garden City, N.Y.: Doubleday, 1982).

W. Gale, ed. *Life in the Universe: The Ultimate Limits to Growth* (Boulder, Col.: Westview Press, 1979).

F. Dyson, *Disturbing the Universe* (New York: Harper and Row, 1979), ch. 11.

MISTY PATCHES IN THE SKY

A good discussion of Babylonian astronomy is given in Otto Neugebauer, *The Exact Sciences in Antiquity* (New York: Dover, 1969).

An excellent history of nebulae is Glyn Jones, *The Search for Nebulae* (Cambridge, England: The Burlington Press, 1975).

Quote from Galileo in *Sidereal Messenger* (1610); translàted in *The Sidereal Messenger of Galileo Galilei* by E. S. Carlos (London, England: Rivingtons, 1880); quote appears also in *The Search for Nebulae,* op. cit., p. 13.

A recent review of the properties of globular clusters is in W. Harris and R. Racine, *Annual Reviews of Astronomy and Astrophysics* (vol. 17, 1979), p. 241. A review of the evolution of globular clusters is A. P. Lightman and S. L. Shapiro, *Reviews of Modern Physics* (vol. 50, 1978), p. 437. An older review suitable for the layperson is I. R. King, *Sky and Telescope* (March 1971), p. 139.

H. Shapley, *Astrophysical Journal* (vol. 48, 1918), p. 89.

Eddington's contributions to stellar structures include the understanding of radiation pressure and transport in stars and the relation between the mass and luminosity of stars. His classic book, summarizing much earlier work, is *The Internal Constitution of Stars* (Cambridge, England: Cambridge University Press, 1926).

Chandrasekhar's contributions to stellar structure include a calculation of the maximum mass obtainable by "white dwarfs." This work is partly summarized in Chandrasekhar's book *An Introduction to the Study of Stellar Structure* (Chicago: University of Chicago Press, 1939).

V. A. Ambartsumian, *Annals of Leningrad State University, Astronomy Series,* (no. 22, 1938), issue 4. Early calculations of the evaporation of stars from star clusters were also done by L. Spitzer, *Monthly Notices of the Royal Astronomical Society* (vol. 100, 1940), p. 396.

I. R. King, *Astronomical Journal* (vol. 63, 1958), p. 114.

Computer simulations of globular clusters were begun by M. Henon, *Bulletin of Astronomy* series 3 (vol. 2, 1967), p. 91; by L. Spitzer and M. H. Hart, *Astrophysical Journal* (vol. 164, 1971), p. 399; and by R. B. Larson, *Monthly Notices of the Royal Astronomical Society* (vol. 147, 1970), p. 323.

The discrepancy between theory and observations has been noted in A. P. Lightman, W. H. Press, and S. Oden-

wald, *Astrophysical Journal* (vol. 219, 1978), p. 629; and
in A. P. Lightman, *Astrophysical Journal Letters* (vol.
263, 1982), p. L19.

Picasso's ideas here come from F. Gilot and C. Lake, *Life
with Picasso* (New York: Avon Books, 1981), pp. 51–
52.

How Long Is a Year?

This essay is based on my paper "A Fundamental Determination of the Planetary Day and Year," *American
Journal of Physics* (March, 1984).

Jonathan Swift, *Gulliver's Travels and Other Writings* (New
York: Bantam Books, 1981), p. 95; first published in
1726.

A recent review of previous work on the determination
of macroscopic scales in terms of fundamental constants (not including the time scales of this essay) is
given in B. J. Carr and M. J. Rees, *Nature* (vol. 278,
1979), pp. 605–612. See also V. F. Weisskopf, *Science*
(vol. 187, 1975), pp. 605–612.

Using various specific assumptions and scenarios, previous
detailed calculations have obtained planetary rotation rates proportional to the maximum rate suggested here. See H. Alfven, *Icarus* (vol. 3, 1964), pp.
57–62; R. T. Giuli, *Icarus* (vol. 8, 1968), pp. 301–323;
A. W. Harris and W. R. Ward, *Annual Review of
Earth and Planetary Science* (vol. 10, 1982), pp. 61–108.

For the newly discovered moon of Pluto, see J. W. Christy
and R. S. Harrington, *Astronomical Journal* (vol. 83,
1978), pp. 1005–1008.

The determination of the "solar constant" (stellar luminosity per unit planetary area) by the requirement of a planetary temperature favorable to life was first pointed out by W. H. Press, *American Journal of Physics* (vol. 48, 1980), pp. 597–598.

For a thorough discussion of the conditions needed to make a planet habitable, with the major emphasis on conditions acceptable to human beings, see S. H. Dole, *Habitable Planets for Man* (New York: American Elsevier, 1970).

For the theoretical relationships between stellar masses and luminosities, see D. D. Clayton, *Principles of Stellar Evolution and Nucleosynthesis* (New York: McGraw-Hill, 1968).

The theoretical arguments suggesting a narrow allowed range for the masses of stars may be found in E. E. Salpeter, *Perspectives in Modern Physics,* R. E. Marshak, ed. (New York: Wiley, 1966), pp. 463–475.

For the observed properties of stars and for planetary data, see C. W. Allen, *Astrophysical Quantities* (London: Athlone Press, 1976).

For a discussion of photochemical reactions and the importance of photosynthesis for life, see G. Wald, *Scientific American* (vol. 201:4, 1959), pp. 92–108.

IRONLAND

This essay received its inspiration from the book *Flatland: A Romance in Many Dimensions,* by Edwin A. Abbott, first published around 1890, reprinted by Dover, New York, in 1952. Abbott's classic concerns a fictitious two-dimensional world, its life and society. His tale hinges on geometry, while mine on physics.

An introduction to the physical basis of magnetism may be found in *Physics,* by D. Halliday and R. Resnick (New York: Wiley, 1967), ch. 37. Somewhat more advanced is the treatment in *Introduction to Solid State Physics,* by C. Kittel (New York: Wiley, 1967).

Five elements—iron, cobalt, nickel, gadolinium, and dysprosium—have the ability of sustaining their own magnetic fields, at sufficiently low temperatures. Magnets made from these elements are called permanent magnets or ferromagnets. Other substances, called paramagnets, may only become magnetic in the presence of other magnets.

The internal magnetic regions I describe are technically called magnetic domains.

The maximum magnetic field achievable by an isolated magnet is called its saturation magnetization. Each of the five ferromagnetic elements listed above has a different saturation magnetization.

The temperature above which a ferromagnet loses its magnetization is called the Curie temperature, named after the French physicist Pierre Curie (1859–1906).

JAM TOMORROW

Pascal and Fermat exchanged letters on the theory of probability in 1654. In the same year, Pascal published his *Traité du triangle arithmetique.* For further information see the entry on Pascal in *Dictionary of Scientific Biography* (New York: Scribners, 1974).

The Tacoma, Washington, residents were questioned by the Environmental Protection Agency on July 12, 1983. See the *New York Times,* July 13, 1983.

For Gilmore references, see, for example, *Time* magazine, November 22, 1976, and January 24, 1977.

Selections from both Graunt's and Halley's works are reprinted in *The World of Mathematics,* Volume 3, James R. Newman, ed. (New York: Simon and Schuster, 1956). Additional biographical information on Halley is given in *Dictionary of Scientific Biography,* op. cit.

Einstein's well-known comment about God playing dice has been paraphrased many times but was first stated in a letter to Max Born on December 12, 1926. See *Einstein, A Centenary Volume,* A. P. French, ed. (Cambridge, Mass.: Harvard University Press, 1979), p. 275.

The statement by Thomas Aquinas may be found in Edmund F. Byrne, *Probability and Opinion* (The Hague, Netherlands: Martinus Nijhoff, 1968), p. 53.

Sindell v. *Abbott Laboratories,* L. A. No. 31063. March 20, 1980. See also *California Law Review* (vol. 69:1179, 1980).

The statement by the White Queen to Alice is in *Through the Looking Glass* by Lewis Carroll, chapter 5.

Index